Praise for th

"*I remember fondly reading* ᴛʜᴇ ʟɪᴏɴ, ᴛʜᴇ ᴡɪᴛᴄʜ, ᴀɴᴅ ᴛʜᴇ Wardrobe *when I was in middle school. The Peaks at the Edge of the World has a similar mix of fantasy and adventure with a moral tale at its center. This is a book that's appropriate for a younger audience than most sci fi/fantasy novels. Enjoy the read!*"

—*Kathy Dunhoff*
ZOLA AWARD-WINNING WOMEN'S FICTION WRITER

"*...a page turner!*" —*Judith Seidel*

"*Ms. Erler puts religion in new settings as she uses the characters in both the past and the future to meld the consequences of a religion lost, then found, then challenged. The ride is exciting. The characters real and engaging.*"

—*Charlene Hecht*
BA MUSIC EDUCATION
LONGTIME WRITER, INCLUDING "GUNSMOKE" FAN FICTION

"*M.F. Erler skillfully pioneers a new writing genre, mixing elements of science fiction, dimensional time-travel, and modern Christian spirituality. She uses likeable characters in well-crafted settings in which we can identify with their real-life struggles.*"

—*Richard Bartlett, MA, PhD*

"*...[M.F.] Erler's book, with its futuristic sci-fi focus and true-to-life grittiness, is not your typical Christian novel. At times, it unabashedly describes the realities of the darkness of humanity in order to contrast it with the power of hope and love found in God's grace. This unique book is well worth your time to read and I highly recommend it.*"

—*Pastor Kevin Bueltmann*
TRINITY LUTHERAN CHURCH - ASSOCIATE PASTOR
TRINITY LUTHERAN CAMP - EXECUTIVE DIRECTOR

Books by M.F. Erler

THE PEAKS SAGA

PEAKS AT THE EDGE OF THE WORLD
Finding the Light

SEARCHING FOR MAIA

MOUNTAINTOPS AND VALLEYS

WHEN THE WORLD GROWS COLD

THE FOUNTAIN AND THE DESERT

BEYOND THE WORLD

WHERE ALL WORLDS END

PEAKS
at the Edge of the
WORLD

M.F. ERLER

PEAKS AT THE EDGE OF THE WORLD, Book 1
Finding the Light
by M.F. Erler

Copyright © 2012, 2018 M.F. Erler
First Edition February 2014
Revised Edition September 2018
All Rights Reserved

Published by

WESTWIND PRESS
an imprint of First Steps Publishing
PO Box 571
Gleneden Beach, Oregon 97388-0571
FirstStepsPublishing.com

ISBN: 978-1-937333-64-5 (hb)
         978-1-937333-61-4 (pb)
         978-1-937333-62-1 (epub)

All lyrics quoted are Public Domain or composed by the author.

Cover illustration by Kabita Studios
Cover design, book formatting by Suzanne Fyhrie Parrott

Please provide feedback

10 9 8 7 6 5 4 3 2

Printed in U.S.A.

THIS BOOK IS DEDICATED TO
MY BELOVED CHILDREN
JONATHAN & EMILIE

Contents

FOREWORD

CHANGE

The world is like a river flowing,
Permanently changing,
Forever running,
Building its own land.

And in the same way,
Changes creep into me, unfelt,
Whirling 'round my feet and head
In eddies.

So my soul
Longs for where I've been,
Craves where I am going,

But it can only be here
in the now.

Why can't I be the river?
At its source—trickling from the deep,
dim in-parts of earth,
At its mouth—wandering slowly, at ease,
before losing itself
in the wholeness of the sea,
And everywhere in between?

M. F. Erler

The answer to this poetic question, of course, is that only God can see the whole river of time at once. But for some reason, he put the desire to see the infinite in his human creatures, as well. It seems that for all my life I've been trying to see beyond the next horizon or over the next ridge, wondering why I seem to ask more about these things than my friends.

That's why this book was written, to help me with my own searching and questions, and perhaps to help others see some of what I occasionally glimpse—just around the next corner—beyond the next planet—or behind the next star.

So yes, this book has been bubbling in my mind for most of my life. Some of the thoughts came to the surface and are printed here, while others are still hiding in the undercurrents of my mental synapses.

Some readers may find it ironic that I write a *book* about a time when all forms of print and writing are considered archaic, and therefore forbidden. I find it no coincidence – in this time I write of – that the primary surviving book is ***The Book***, the one bearing this as its only title.

Perhaps this is because throughout my life this Book had a central influence on my thinking, even though it was not commonly read in my home when I was a child. Somehow, I just kept being drawn to it. Oh, I have questioned it! And I've read many other books and opinions. But none of them seemed to reach deep down into my psyche like this Book does—none have the same ring of truth and authority.

I would be lying if I didn't say that many inspirations for *The Peaks at the Edge of the World* have come during moments of studying The Book. Flashes of insight seem to come suddenly and feel similar to descriptions I've heard from those who meditate.

Please understand I make *no claims* to be 'spiritually enlightened' or 'inspired by God'! All I am is a humble mouthpiece, trying with my own stumbling words to relate things I feel have been shown to me. Like Eli in the Desert, I am just a voice...

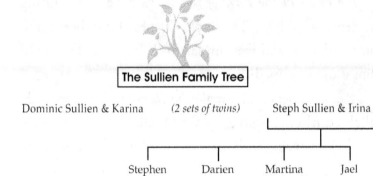

The Sullien Family Tree

Dominic Sullien & Karina *(2 sets of twins)* Steph Sullien & Irina

Stephen   Darien   Martina   Jael

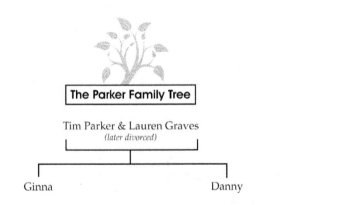

The Parker Family Tree

Tim Parker & Lauren Graves
(later divorced)

Ginna   Danny

CHAPTER 1

PROLOGUE

Dominic Sullien stood in the center of a large meadow, letting his eyes rove across the scene. The wild grasses were a brilliant green in this season and exceptionally tall. He didn't even have to bend down to run his hands across their tops. As he walked slowly through them, he felt the slight tickle as they brushed the palms of his hands.

The sun was warm on his face before he turned his back to it. The sight that met his eyes took his breath away. Of course, he'd seen The Peaks many times in his life, but something in the lighting today made them seem to move closer to him in a sudden leap. There was still snow on the highest crags, and the rising sun—behind him now—was etching every ridge in sharp contrast to its neighbor, against the deep blue sky of planet Terres.

With only one settlement on this planet, no one bothered naming these landmarks yet. They were just

'The Peaks' to everyone in Terres-City. Besides, few people ventured out of the City—like he and his brother did.

Now he could see Steph striding toward him, also brushing his hands through the grass stems. Anyone seeing them would take a second look, for they were identical twins. Both had the lean, muscular look of youth, striking green eyes, and curly blond hair that ruffled now in the stiff breeze.

"They look amazing today, don't they, Dominic?" His brother indicated the mountain range with a tilt of his head.

Dominic nodded, "I can see why people who are tired of the stilted life of the City could want to try to live out here, Steph."

"I suppose. But how can people really survive? What's there to eat? Where can they find shelter?"

He shrugged. They both heard the rumors of refugees who deserted the City and the Council's System to live in the Wilds. But neither of them had ever seen any evidence to prove it—so far.

He admitted, though, there were times when his spirit chafed at the rigidity of the System and the Council's iron-fisted rules. From their mother, they heard stories of the True King, who supposedly ruled with peace, wisdom, and freedom on mankind's ancestral planet, Earth. This was something never taught in the System Schools, though. Was it real, or only a myth?

If he was honest with himself, though, he admitted he did have a yearning deep inside to try to escape to the freedom and hope his mother talked of. But how? Sure, they'd learned to make these brief escapes from the City, by crossing the GAP. But these were merely a temporary respite.

Now he turned to his brother. "Should we practice crossing the GAP again?"

Steph nodded eagerly. "I think I can do it by myself this time. Why do you think it works for me? After all, you're the one who was born first."

"Perhaps it's because we're identical twins, Steph. We have the same genes. So, where are you going to take me?"

There was a sudden twinkle in Steph's eyes. "It's a surprise."

Now Steph took his brother's hands in his, closing his eyes slowly, a look of intense concentration on his face.

Dominic felt the sudden moment of vertigo only GAP-crossers could feel. The ground seemed to fall away beneath him, and then suddenly his feet were resting on firm pavement. By the sounds in his ears, he knew they were back in the City, but there was also a sound of splashing water nearby.

"Don't open your eyes yet," came Steph's voice. "See if you can guess where we are."

He smiled to himself. Steph was really enjoying his new-found ability. "Well, I think I hear a fountain, but we're in the City, so I guess we're near a park."

He felt his brother's hands on his shoulders, turning him to face slightly to the right.

"Okay, you can open your eyes now."

When he first opened them, the light seemed much too bright, and he blinked. Yes, there was the large fountain in the city's central park, and behind it he could see the towering, needle-like structure of Neptune Spire.

Seated on a bench beside the fountain were two dark-haired young women. It didn't take more than a glance to see they were twins. He let out a soft whistle.

"Like my surprise?" whispered Steph.

He nodded. Twins weren't common on Terres, and these two were very pretty. "How did you find them?"

"I'm not sure how it works, but I seem to be able to focus on people, as well as places, when I cross the GAP. So I can find certain people, even if I don't know their exact location."

He stared at Steph in disbelief. This was something even the Star Corps training never mentioned. "But where did you meet them?"

"Oh, I've just been doing some research," he grinned.

Yes, Steph was the more serious and studious of them. While he was more likely to be out conversing with people, Steph preferred to work on the Terminal in their sleeping room. This was the only Terminal in their home, though most people in the City had several.

But often, Steph would go instead to the antique books hidden in the back closet. Few people owned books anymore, and there were rumors the Council might be outlawing them soon.

"So, what do you think of them, Dominic?"

"Nice," he smiled. "Which one do you like?"

"Oh, the one with the long, single braid in her hair," said Steph.

Now he noticed that one of the young women had two braids in her shining, dark hair, while her sister's was in one fishscale-style braid hanging down her back.

"Okay, Steph. You can have first pick, even though I'm the eldest," he chuckled. "After all, you found them, and they both look beautiful to me."

"Yeah, I'm wondering whether we could even tell them apart if their hair was the same. By the way, Dominic, yours is named Karina—mine is Irina."

Five Standard Years later, Steph and Irina Sullien brought their first son into the world. They named him Stephen, in honor of his father. Three more children were to bless their home before the darker forces of the System began to close in around them.

CHAPTER 2

STRANGE VISITORS

"Teacher's Pet!"

"Yeah! What a nerd!"

Ginna Parker could hear the taunting voices of the fourth graders all the way at her end of the playground. And she knew who they were directed at, even before she heard the next words:

"Danny is a dork—just like his sister!"

'Just like me,' she thought and felt her eyes begin to sting. 'Oh, don't cry, silly,' she told herself, getting even angrier. 'Crying never helped anything. They'll just laugh at you, too, like they always do.'

As she thought, she was working her way slowly around the corner of the school to where she could see the elementary playground. She knew she wasn't supposed to be over there. Eighth graders weren't allowed in the third to fifth-grade section. But in spite of herself, she worked her way to the edge of the forbidden playground, telling herself she just needed to check on what was happening.

There was Danny, his pale brown hair wafting in a slight breeze, sitting on a swing and pushing slowly with his feet. Suddenly one of the boys rushed toward him, shouting, "Hey, outta my way! I was playing on this!"

Before Danny could move, the boy grabbed the swing and pulled it out from under him. Ginna heard the loud crack as her brother's head hit the hard ground. The next thing she knew she was running toward the bigger boy, fists flying. She landed one punch to his head before he even knew what hit him.

"Stop that!" She heard a booming voice behind her. "What's going on here?"

Without even looking, she knew it was the school principal, Mr. Jackson.

"He pushed Danny!" she heard her voice shout in reply.

"Yeah, Danny never fights for himself," other voices taunted.

She'd already raised her fist to land another blow when a large hand grabbed her from behind.

"That's enough!" said Mr. Jackson gruffly. "You shouldn't be on this side of the school ground, and you know it."

Ginna could feel her cheeks beginning to flush bright red. Her head continued to throb with anger, as the principal continued, "I want to see you in my office right now. And Danny, too. Help him clean up, and be quick about it."

She swallowed the shout in her throat and just nodded silently.

Danny was sitting up now, rubbing his head and looking up at her with dark green eyes, through his mussed and dusty brown hair.

"Are you all right?" she asked, kneeling beside him.

He nodded, then whispered, "Thanks, Ginna. I'm sorry I got you in trouble, though."

"Well, I couldn't just stand by and let that bully beat you up."

Danny nodded again and tried to smile.

"Do you want to wash your face on the way to Mr. Jackson's office?"

"Yeah."

Ginna took his hand. While she helped her brother at the water fountain, and as they walked up the staircase to the office, her mind began to struggle with what to tell the principal.

'It's not our fault nobody likes us,' she could say. 'We can't help it if we're from Texas, and they say we talk funny. In Texas, nobody said that. Besides, we never wanted to move to Colorado anyway. It's only because our father-'

No this would be too hard. She knew if she tried to talk about Dad, the tears would flood over. She still didn't want to believe what her mother said was true—that their father wouldn't ever come home again. Then all the words seemed to just melt out of her mind as they stood in the doorway of the office, and Mr. Jackson looked up.

"Come in," he said, and his voice didn't seem quite as gruff as it did outside.

There were no other chairs other than the one the principal was using, so they stood in front of his desk.

"Now, tell me what happened, Ginna."

"Well," she began, "The fifth graders were teasing Danny and saying he was a nerd and teacher's pet, just like me. I walked over to see what was happening. Then that big boy—I don't even know his name—pushed Danny out of the swing. He hit his head on the ground so hard, I could hear it from where I was. Next thing I knew I was over there, and-"

"Yes, I saw that part," Mr. Jackson nodded, and there seemed to be a calming tone in his voice. "Are you all right, Danny?"

"Yes, sir."

"You should have come and told me or a teacher instead of fighting, Ginna."

"But I was afraid Danny might have a concussion," she protested. "And he needs me. I mean, we're all alone here, and we have to stick together. Nobody likes us."

Mr. Jackson was silent for a moment as he looked down at his desk. "I realize you've had some hard times, and it's difficult to adjust to such a new place and a new school."

"And our dad leaving, too," Danny added softly.

Ginna was surprised he said this and suddenly felt ashamed, staring at the floor to hide her burning cheeks.

"Yes, I know it's difficult," the principal's voice went on. "Deer Path is a small town. People here just aren't used to newcomers. They don't know how to react. Just give them time. And try not to let the teasing make you angry."

"That's impossible," Ginna mumbled, hoping her voice wouldn't crack to reveal the tears she felt welling up.

"Well, it's the best we can do for now," he replied. "I'll talk to those boys, too. So let's give it one more try, okay?"

They both nodded slowly.

"Okay, you two need to go to your classrooms now."

As they walked back down the stairs, Ginna whispered, "That advice was no help."

Danny seemed as though he hadn't even heard her. "I've got something I need to tell you after school. There's no time now." Then they were at the door of his classroom. "See you then, Ginna," he said and even smiled.

When Danny was gone, she suddenly felt very alone, the way she felt most of the time, lately. Danny was her only friend since they'd moved. It didn't matter at all that they were almost four years apart in age. There was just something special between them. She didn't really want to be with anyone else.

Besides, everyone else teased her for being too tall and skinny, or for being too smart in her subjects. "Smarty Pants!" or "Beanpole!" were phrases she heard often, and sometimes the speaker didn't even bother to whisper.

She knew how it would be as soon as she walked into the classroom, the sidelong glances and outright leers. She paused with her hand on the knob, wondering if she could face this again, but knew she had no choice. All she could do was get through the rest of the afternoon. Then she could be with Danny again, and they could go home.

At last three o'clock came. As she and Danny walked off the hard-packed clay of the school grounds to the dusty streets of Deer Path, Colorado, she could hardly wait to hear what he wanted to tell her.

When they were far enough away from the other kids, he finally spoke, "You didn't tell Mr. Jackson the worst part."

"What?" She'd expected him to say something else.

"The worst part of the teasing."

"Oh, you mean how they ridicule us for going to church and Sunday School?"

Danny nodded.

"I didn't think he'd understand," she said.

"I guess not. But it bothers me more to be called 'Bible-boy' than 'nerd'," he said.

This reminded her of other taunting words, "If you're such good people, how come your parents got a divorce?"

'That cuts the deepest,' she thought, 'Because there's no good reply.'

"I wish we could have stayed in Texas," Danny said. "I don't like Colorado."

"Mom had to come here to work. You know that, Danny. This was the best job she could find right now."

She heard her mother's words echo in her mind, 'They need a public relations expert at a nuclear power plant. It's the best opportunity for me around.' So here they were in Eastern Colorado, whether they liked it or not.

By this time, they'd reached the small gray house where they lived now. "It's just until we can afford something better," Mom always said.

The house was empty as they went in. Mom wouldn't be home for at least two more hours. They opened a can of soda to share and pulled out the last of the corn chips. Then they settled on the rickety old back porch where they could look out from the edge of town, across the fields and farms to the west. Through a shimmering haze, they could barely see the peaks of the Rocky Mountains far across the plains.

"Those mountains look like they're painted on the horizon," she mused. "Almost like they're unreal."

"Yeah, they look like they're the edge of the world, and nothing is beyond them."

Ginna wondered at the poetry of his words. Danny always seemed to find just the perfect way to describe things. She should be used to his ways by now, how he always seemed beyond his ten years.

One of his teachers in Texas told Mom she thought he had a photographic memory. It did seem he remembered everything he read, word-for-word. Ever since he learned to read, he always seemed to have a book in front of him. His favorites were the encyclopedias. Dinner conversations usually involved Danny telling what he learned from his day's reading.

"I feel like we're living near the end of the world," he was saying then. "Or maybe the edge of time. Like something strange could happen any moment. It's weird."

She stopped with the soda halfway to her mouth. Why was her heart pounding suddenly at his words? Was there a deeper meaning inside them, beyond the over-ripe imaginations of two lonely children? She seemed to get this heart-pounding feeling more here in Colorado. And now she could see a new and strange light shining in her little brother's eyes.

He seemed to be looking right through her. She groped for something to say, anything to calm this fear welling up inside her.

"You said you needed to tell me something after school," she managed to whisper.

He nodded silently, still looking at her. But the light in his eyes didn't fade, and a long time passed before he finally spoke. "I've been having dreams," he said softly.

"Again? Like the ones before, where you saw the future, and Dad leaving?"

"No, different from those." He took a deep breath and silence flitted between them. "I dreamed I met someone tall and handsome, with blond hair and shining eyes," he continued at last. "At first I thought it was Dad. But it was someone else. I don't know who. He said he heard me, and that he's coming to help."

"Help us? How?"

"I don't know."

"Who was it?"

"I don't know that either. But, Ginna, he seemed so kind and strong, and even beautiful. I really hope I do meet him for real."

"People have a right to say we're both crazy!" she said suddenly to cover the fear that was returning. "You for your dreams, and me for listening to them."

"I can't help it," he said evenly, and his eyes were shining brighter than ever now. "I just know inside me that they're not ordinary dreams."

Ginna's heart was pounding now. She wanted to believe her brother but was afraid to. It was all too strange. Things like this happened only in books, not in real life.

Maybe Danny was reading too much. She shook her head to try to clear it.

Just then, there came an urgent sound in her ears. She jumped up and realized the phone was ringing. Thankful for something else to think about, she rushed through the back door and grabbed the phone. As quick as lightning, her thoughts flashed, 'It's bad enough not to be able to afford any cell phones, but why can't we at least have a cordless phone in the house?'

"Hello?" she said into the receiver.

"Ginna? It's Mom, are you two all right?"

"Just fine, Mom."

"Listen, Honey, I'm sorry, but something's come up here we have to finish tonight, an important news release. So, I'll be here an hour or two later. Can you get some supper for yourself and Danny?"

"Sure, Mom."

"Just fix a can of soup or some hot dogs. And don't forget to lock the door as soon as it gets dark."

"Okay, Mom."

"I'll get home as soon as I can. 'Bye for now. Love you."

"'Bye, Mom. Love you, too."

She waited to hear the phone click before she hung up. That was no help. She hated to be without an adult in the house when it got dark. Of course, she'd never admit that to anyone, feeling she was too old to be afraid of the dark.

"What was that?" Danny asked as she went back out to the porch.

"Oh, Mom's going to be late, so I have to fix us supper."

He made no reply as she sat down next to him on the stoop, and followed his gaze across the plains toward the hazy peaks to the west.

"I hope we get to see those mountains up close someday."

"Mom said we would when she gets time off."

"That'll be a long time, I think," she shrugged.

The afternoon sun was sinking lower now, making everything deepen in color. Shimmering waves of heat seemed to be rising from the fields. The old out-building and windmill in the distance began to look unreal, as though they were about to fade into the haze. Farther past them the heat waves seemed to take on shapes before her eyes.

There! It looked like two figures walking toward them. One was tall and handsome, the other much short-er, both with blond hair that seemed to shine brighter than the sun. But they couldn't be real. It must be a mirage. If she blinked they'd disappear.

Hadn't she already blinked several times? She covered her eyes with her hand, but when she looked again, they were still there, moving closer toward them. Suddenly Danny grabbed her hand hard.

"Ouch!" she cried. "What is it?"

"It's my dream! At least the tall one. He's the one I saw."

They found themselves standing on the porch now, hand in hand. The sun suddenly got brighter, bathing the area all around them in a blinding white light. She opened her mouth to speak, but the words froze somewhere in her throat. All she could do was stand there, gripping Danny's hand. Her mind wanted to ask, 'Is this real? What does this mean?' But even now, her thoughts seemed paralyzed deep inside her.

Soon the light was so bright she could barely see at all. She wanted to close her eyes but found her eyelids stuck. Then came the voice. It was very deep and strong, yet also soothing. She felt the light begin to fade, and cool darkness flowed over her like water.

"We've come as you called, Daniel." She began to make out words. "We know the trials you face and have come to help as much as we can."

Then came the sound of singing and beautiful music, like bright water dancing in a fountain. She felt her heart lighten and her mind begin to unfreeze. Soon beautiful colors were swirling before her eyes, and she began floating, suspended on something soft and warm.

CHAPTER 3

THE GAP-CROSSERS

She woke with a start to find she was in the dark.

"Danny!" she cried. How had she gone to sleep? She had to lock the door.

As she rose, she realized she was on their living room sofa.

"It's all right, Ginna," came Danny's voice. "I'm right here. We're safe with Jon."

She sat up blinking. "Jon? Who's he?"

"He's the friend I saw in my dream."

Danny took her hand, and she could see him pointing across to a chair. Then she saw a candle burning on the table, the tall blond beside it. He was smiling at her, his eyes shining the way Danny's often did. They were a strange color, too deep for brown, but not at all black.

"Hello, Ginna," he said softly. "I'm Jon, son of Jakol. And I *am* a friend."

She found herself nodding, something in the tone of his voice reassuring her.

"Jon and his friend came to us from the future," Danny's voice said.

'That's impossible!' The words welled up in her mind, but Jon's eyes were still shining at her, seeming to look through her, and no sound came from her lips.

"This is my friend Jael Sullien," Jon's voice said then.

She blinked and realized another chair was pulled close to the coffee table, where a younger man sat, smiling at her. His hair was blond, too, but longer and curlier than Jon's, and his eyes were a pale color like watery green. He seemed much smaller, perhaps her own age, though age was something vague when she looked at these two. They seemed beyond such things somehow. The way the light of the candle danced in their eyes and on their hair made them both seem full of some rich life, something magical. And the more she looked at them, the smaller and plainer she felt, with her own pale brown eyes and short, mousy hair.

"You may light the lamp now, Jael," said Jon.

She and Danny watched in silence as the young man took a strange lantern they'd never seen before and began to turn a dial on it. Soon a warm yellow light began to flow from its fluted chimney. The light spread slowly around the room, almost as though it were flowing like thick honey, golden in warm sunlight. The base of the lamp was so close to the same color it looked liquid, too, and the chimney glowed with shadowy designs of swirls and flowing shapes.

Ginna began to feel warm and comfortable inside, her fear flowing away in the honey-colored light.

"Should we explain the GAP to them, Jon?" Jael asked, speaking for the first time. Ginna found she liked the sound of his voice very much.

"I doubt they'll understand," Jon replied.

"Oh, please!" cried Danny suddenly. "Please explain! We want to try to understand."

A broad smile appeared on Jon's face. "Very well," he said. He took a deep breath and began, "As I told you, Daniel, we come from the future, as you see time now. In your future, there will be a great upheaval, and after that a renewal of understanding and knowledge, and the reign of the True King. Then the power of the firstborn to cross the Galactic Antipaterminal Passage—the GAP—will be discovered. Or perhaps I should say rediscovered because it was known at some time in Earth's ancient past."

"The power of the firstborn?" Ginna found herself asking. Danny's hand squeezed hers tightly. "Does this mean I have some kind of power?"

"If you're firstborn, you have the ability to learn," Jon smiled. "But it's not recognized or understood in your time. And often it takes the understanding of the lastborn to develop its full potential." He glanced from Jael to Danny with a smile dancing in his eyes.

"This power is very complex," Jon went on, "But to put it simply, it's the ability to cross gaps of space or time in an instant, a way of cutting across the four dimensions."

"In geometry, we learned only three dimensions," Ginna found herself saying.

Jon chuckled. "Oh no, there are many more than three. Even in your time, many people talk of Time as the fourth dimension."

"Oh, I forgot," she mumbled, feeling foolish. "I'm sorry. Please go on."

"Actually, people used the first three dimensions in the beginning, and the GAP-crossers learned to cut across vast distances of space to new stars and planets, which the people of Earth colonized. Our home planet, Terres, was one such colony. But later, scientists discovered that when great GAPs of space were crossed, time was altered, too. We were traveling forward in time as we crossed each GAP, without knowing it. Then, in our century, a few of us learned how to reverse this effect and travel backward in time. But going back is much more difficult and dangerous."

"You're time-travelers?" Ginna asked in disbelief. 'Am I dreaming this?'

"GAP-crossers, to be more exact," Jon said. "It's being explored by scientists in our time, though few have perfected it fully. Jael and I together have a special chemistry neither of us has apart. Perhaps that's what you and Daniel have. Otherwise he couldn't have called us."

Danny squeezed her hand and whispered, "I called them." It wasn't a question.

"Our initial data indicate Daniel and Jael have great genetic similarities."

"Genetic? You mean their genes, their heredity?" she asked. "How can that be when you're so-"

"So far removed in space and time?"

She nodded.

"This has been a mystery for many generations. We know there's historical evidence in all eras and times of such similarities, of forerunners. But there's still much to learn in this area."

"I've heard people say they feel they've lived another life before this one," Danny said. "Is this what they mean by reincarnation?"

"Reincarnation is a mistaken way to describe it," Jael replied. "Each of us has only our own single life to live."

"But," Jon added, "Some do sense a kindred spirit, or forerunner, from their past. It's not the same as what your world calls reincarnation, though."

"Really?" Ginna was looking from Danny to Jael. "You two are different people, from different worlds, but somehow very similar, too?"

"That's the best explanation we can give for now," said Jon. "Perhaps later we can explore this more with you." He smiled at Ginna, and she felt her cheeks begin to blush.

"But what does this have to do with us right now?" Danny asked.

"We've come to answer your call for help," said Jon, his voice even deeper now. "We hope, with the similarities between you and Jael, that as you hear our story, you'll find answers for yourselves. Are you willing to enter the GAP and to experience our lives with us?"

"Yes," Danny said, after a long silence. Ginna merely nodded.

"Very well. Jael, you may begin."

Jael's voice seemed to take on a musical tone when he spoke again, his words rising and falling around them like a chant. When Ginna looked at the lantern, she saw brown shapes swirling rapidly and beginning to take on forms of people and buildings.

CHAPTER 4

A STORY FROM ANOTHER TIME

You might say this story took place very far away *[Jael's voice said]*. But it's best for you to think of it in the distant future, for past and future are related. Perhaps time is a circle, after all.

Now that we've learned to cross Time GAPs as well, we can come to tell you our story. We hope as you experience it with us, you'll find what we've found—the center of this circle of time, the only strong place in the Universe. Perhaps when we're finished, you'll see this story isn't as faraway—past or future—as you thought. It's really wherever you are, because it will soon be part of you, as it's part of us.

You may think I'm too young to be telling this, but it's been a long time—and many times—since I was the young boy in this story. Then, you say, how can you remember it so well? I can't say for sure. But I know somehow, I've reached a point in the circle where I can look back across and see some things as clearly as if they were only yesterday:

At the very start of my life, I see dimly lit windows of the room where I slept, so there must have been some kind of lights outside. There was the cool of the sheets, and my father's voice singing me to sleep with gentle songs. He rubbed my back in great, sweeping circles as he sang:

"O Danny Boy, the pipes the pipes are calling. . ."

[*"That's a song my father used to sing to me!" Danny exclaimed.*

"Well, I did say we were very similar," Jael smiled.]

This is the only memory I have of my father. For by the time I was old enough to be aware of him, he was gone. But that comes later.

There's a memory of listening to words coming in on the transceiver, while I stared at the covers of books on a shelf, memorizing their colors and patterns. That's what most of those first memories are—colors, patterns, and textures, like the feel of the rug on the floor or the paint on the wall. Or the light making patterns in the room as I sat on my mother's lap and listened to her soft voice reading or singing to me.

At first, the only thing I understood was the calm, soothing sound of her voice. Then there were words here and there. And as I grew, these words became stories. The story I remember most vividly, from the very first, is the one about Daniel—

[*"A story about me?" Danny asked incredulously.*

"No, the one about Daniel in the Lions' Den," Jael chuckled.

"Oh, you mean the Bible story!" Ginna said. "The Bible was still around then?"

"Yes," said Jael. "But not many still had one. We just called it 'The Book,' which is what the word 'Bible' actually means."]

Anyway, I was impressed that Daniel was so brave, *[Jael resumed]*. He never doubted his God would take care of him. My mother seemed to tell this story to me more often than others. It wasn't until much later I began to realize why it was so important for me to know.

Of course, these were all just tales to me then, like the ones my brothers told me about beasts in the wilds and feier-cats. The world of a child is full of stories which are real and unreal simultaneously.

The most vivid memory from that early time is one of fear and wonder. I must have been quite small, for it's the first time I remember waking up alone in the night. It was as dark as nothingness, a total void, like nothing I'd ever felt before. The darkness was something I could reach out and touch. It engulfed me, and I felt as though I were choking.

Somehow, I was out of my bed and groping along the wall. The door should be here—where was it? Why had it disappeared? My hand found only the smooth paint of the wall. My heart was pounding, and I remember vividly thinking, 'Is this what it's like to be dead?' Then a piercing cry filled the blackness, and I was lying on the floor trembling.

Suddenly a beam of brilliant light gleamed across the floor. It seemed to flood the room, pushing all the black into the corners. But more than that, it flowed into my heart. I had light and hope! I was alive again! Then I felt my mother's arms around me, and I was sobbing and clinging to her.

"Jael, what's the matter?" she asked, rocking me.

"It was so dark. I thought I was dead. Then somebody screamed."

"That was you, honey. But it's okay now. Momma's here and there's no need to be afraid."

From then on, I believed light was the thing that could save me from anything.

As I grew, the images began to sort themselves into patterns. I knew the face of my mother first, and later learned her name was Irina Sullien. I also had two older brothers, Stephen and Darien. Stephen had the light-colored hair, and Darien's was dark. And there was another with dark hair, but it was longer like my mother's. This was Martina, my sister.

Our house was on two levels connected by a spiral staircase. Below was a large area with soft floors and cushions, and near it the place Mother called the galley, where the wonderful smells of food came from. There was a flat raised place where we knelt or sat to eat. Beyond the galley was a sunny, glass-roofed place where all kinds of plants grew in pots and bottles of colored liquids. It was warm in there, and I loved to sit in the light. Sometimes, when Mother was preparing a meal, she'd give me a sample of some food to nibble.

Martina would laugh and say, "Mother, you spoil that boy!"

Mother would reply, "You had your spoiling when you were his age. He's the only little one I have now."

We did most things together in the house, playing games with bits of colored plastic and large sheets of paperboard. Those were the days I liked best, when we were all together. By this time, Father was gone long enough that I had very little memory of him. Sometimes, Martina and Darien would talk about him, when they thought Mother couldn't hear them. Once I caught her standing in a doorway behind them, listening with tears gleaming in her eyes.

Most days, though, everyone was gone except Mother and me. Then the house was still and lonely. Sometimes, we'd go out and walk in the open air, looking at other houses along the way, while little groundcars hummed past on the street. We didn't have a groundcar of our own, but I could see them parked beside many of the houses near ours. From the front of each extended a large cord which hooked into the wall of the house.

One day I noticed there was an outlet in our house. "Why don't we have a groundcar?" I asked Mother.

"We used to, but when your father went away to the wars, we sold it," she replied. "We can take the Tube anywhere we need to go now."

My favorite part of the day was when the others came home. Martina and Darien always came first. Then Stephen would arrive just when the food was ready.

As we ate, there would be much talking and usually laughter. But sometimes their voices were deep and quiet. I remember the words well, though I didn't completely understand them, when one time Martina said, "It's so hard!"

"I know, Honey," Mother said, quietly. "But we must do what we believe is right. We know The Book is truth, no matter what they tell you in school."

"But why do we have to be so different—reading old books, instead of having Terminals, or growing our own food, and doing things alone, instead of in the Neighborhood Centers? No wonder I don't have any friends."

"We have fun together, though, don't we Martina?" Stephen said.

She nodded but didn't look up.

"It's not just that," Darien added. "It's the way people say, 'You mean you actually believe those old tales about gods? Those are just myths. We know better now. How can you be so old-fashioned?' "

"I know," said Stephen, "I always hated the way the Tutor would look at me when he said something he knew I didn't believe. It was like he *wanted* me to argue with him."

About this time, Mother nodded. "I know it's hard for you. But you must remember two things. First, old ways are not bad just because they're old—no matter what they tell you at school. Second, your father, Steph, and I knew we couldn't force you to follow our ways. All we want is to give you *all* the truth, not just the half the Council allows to be taught. We hope and pray that with the whole truth, you'll make right choices as they come to you."

Her eyes looked troubled as she said these words, and she seemed to be seeing something very distant, especially when she spoke of Father. I began to understand that Father was far away in a dangerous place.

Each night, just before we went to bed, she or Stephen took down the ancient black book from a special shelf. Martina and Darien made sure the windows were all tightly shuttered, so no outside light came into the room. Then one of them read us words from the Book, words like ones Mother read to me when we were alone. After that, all of us closed our eyes while Stephen said words out of his head—called prayers.

"Close your eyes, Jael," Mother smiled. "We're going to talk to God now."

I wondered, "How can we talk to someone we can't see?"

"We can feel him in our hearts," she replied.

I still wasn't sure I understood all this, but I could tell it was important to them.

As I said, I now knew our father was far away. When they thought I was old enough, my brothers told me he was at the Galactic Wars, where men must go to keep us safe. But I wanted him *home,* to keep us safe here. It seemed a strange way to protect us—to go faraway, and leave us alone and fearful. I was especially sad because I couldn't even remember what his face looked like.

After awhile, I got used to being alone with Mother. She would sing as she worked, and I liked the sound. She sang the most when she was cooking special things for what she called "Festival Natale."

"No one celebrates this anymore," she told me. "It came from our ancient ancestors. For us, it's a special memorial of when our King came to Earth for the first time."

"Mother, what's Earth?"

"It's the original home of humankind, but they refuse to teach of it in the schools. Anyway, when the King first came, he didn't come as royalty at all. He was born in a stable."

"What's a stable?" I asked.

"A place where animals live."

"But why would a person be born there, instead of a house?"

"He wanted to be like the poor, lowly people who had no homes," she smiled.

"That's strange," I said. "What made him a king, then?"

"The Book says he was God's son, and he brought a special message of love to people on Earth."

"Is this really a true story?"

"Your father always said it as true, Jael, and I believe it. This is what makes us different from other people here on Terres. Stephen will read the whole story from The Book tonight, the way your father used to."

And he did. After Mother made sure the windows were well-shaded, he read from the ancient Book about how a baby was born, and angels from the sky told some people tending sheep all about it.

"Glory to God in the highest," he read. "And on Earth, peace, goodwill toward men."

"What are angels?" I asked.

"Beings who serve the True Lord," said Martina. "But they're not human like us. They can fly, it's said."

Then Stephen added, "Those sheep-herders went to see the baby those angels told them about, and then they spread the news to everyone around."

"Did they sing songs, like we do?"

"I'm sure they did, Jael," he said. "Should we sing one now?"

"Okay."

I remember the songs best from this time, though sometimes I get the words mixed up. The tunes still ring in my mind, and I'm sure they helped plant the seeds that would grow into understanding as I grew older.

It came upon a midnight clear
That glorious song of old,
From angels bending near the earth
To touch their harps of gold.

Peace on the earth, goodwill to men,
The blessed angels sing ...
Let all the earth give back the song,
Which now the angels sing.

***

One morning, Stephen met my eyes when I woke instead of Mother, something which had never happened before. His eyes looked very wet and sad, too.

"Come on, little guy," he said. "I'll give you a ride down."

As we went down the stairs, I was high on his shoulders, where I could see Mother sitting on a cushion by the window. She was very still and staring at something held limply in her hand. In the galley, I saw Darien's eyes were red, and Martina's cheeks were very wet. They thought I wouldn't understand, but I already knew.

"Jael-" someone started to say.

"I know," I said hoarsely. "Father isn't coming home."

"No. Not now—or ever again," whispered Stephen. "He's been killed in the war."

The house was very quiet most of the time after that. The light didn't dance in the rooms like before. And though she tried, Mother hardly ever sang to me again.

CHAPTER 5

THE SILENT TIME

The time passing after this was quiet, like the stillness of the house. Not the quiet of peace, but the tension of silence. The days tried to pass as before, but somehow things were never the same again. Oh, Mother still read to me sometimes, and we'd even take short walks on sunny days. But her voice had lost something. There was no smile in it anymore.

I was growing, though I wasn't aware of it, more quickly in my mind than my body. It didn't seem at all strange to me when I began to read many of the words in the books I pulled down from the shelf. I heard more of the conversations around me than anyone guessed.

"Jael seems to understand more than I remember doing when I was his age," Stephen said one day.

"Maybe you just don't remember when you were that age," Darien chuckled.

"I do!" Martina piped in. "Jael is special, that's all. Perhaps there's a unique plan for him, and he has special powers."

"We shouldn't talk too much of this," Mother said in a voice full of quiet tension. "We can't know why Jael is as he is. Perhaps he even understands what we're saying right now. It may be the 'special things' ahead for him won't be easy or good. He may be given special strength to face very hard times to come."

No one replied. The room around us seemed to vibrate with some strange frequency that mingled with the evening light as it faded into the corners.

When the sun set, they closed the shades at all the windows and Stephen read to us from the ancient black Book. Some nights we sat and talked about what he read to us. But this time, he just closed the Book when he was finished and sat in silence.

Not long after this, the stranger came. No one was home except Mother and me. By now, I knew it was too early for my brothers and sister to come home. No one else had ever stopped and knocked at our door before, so Mother's eyes seemed bright with fear as she opened it for the stranger.

He was a funny-looking man, short and pudgy. His hair was very thin on top of his large, round head. He wore shiny spectacles on his smooth, white face and smiled a thin-lipped little smile as he nodded to her, "Good day, Ma'am. I am from your Neighbor Improvement Committee."

Mother motioned for him to come in, though no stranger had ever been in our house. What's more, I can't seem to remember what he and Mother said, though I was used to listening to and understanding conversations by this time. They spoke in softly droning voices, while the stranger's eyes roamed around the room, seeming to miss nothing.

Then he was gone.

But Mother just sat staring into space for the rest of the day. I couldn't even get her to talk to me, so I sat on a small chair in silence and practiced writing the letters she'd been teaching me.

I wondered if I should say anything to Stephen or Darien when they came home, but Mother did it for me.

"A Questioner came today," she said, as we were seated around the table at the evening meal.

Stephen's eyes darted toward me.

"He questioned only me," she added quickly.

"What about?"

"I don't remember," she sighed. "I guess he put me in a trance."

"You're sure he didn't bother Jael?" Martina asked.

Mother shook her head. Now I could see tears in her eyes. "I'm sorry if I've failed you."

Stephen took her hand in his, and gently stroked her shoulder with his other hand. "You've done the best you could, Mother."

"I *have* failed you, and your dear father," she moaned.

"Please don't, Mother!" Martina was crying now, too.

Darien's hands were gripping the table fiercely as though he might crack it. He seemed to want to speak, but he kept shaking his head instead.

"No matter what happens," said Stephen, "Please remember we love you, Mother."

The rest of us just stared at the two of them, not knowing what to say.

***

The next time strangers came was a few days later. This time there were two of them, tall and bulky men. All of us were home that day, and I was glad Stephen was there because these men had hard-looking faces and big voices which echoed around the room.

We were all seated in the front room of the house, with Mother between the men. She never spoke a word, and as the men talked to Stephen, she seemed to shrink into a smaller and smaller space. Darien was standing by the front window, staring out as though he didn't want to listen to their words. Martina was close beside me, and she often squeezed my hand until it began to hurt. Some of the words they said still ring in my mind:

"She must be rehabilitated," one of the men said. "She's lost touch with reality, with rationality. All she seems to do is teach this child the myths of ancient books." He seemed to almost sneer as he said these last words. "The child should be taught the ways of Terres, his world, not tales of some mythical place from another time."

Stephen nodded but didn't speak. Martina shifted me onto her lap and put her arms around me.

"She will be taken to the Institute for rehabilitation. She's agreed to this."

Mother was sitting with a blank stare in her eyes. I wasn't sure how she could have agreed or disagreed with anything. A sharp sound came from the corner where Darien was standing, but Stephen made a hand sign to him, and he turned back to looking out the window.

Then the men stood, pulling Mother up with them. Suddenly I knew they were taking her away, and a great sob began to well up inside me. I buried my head in Martina's shoulder.

"You must see the child receives proper instruction," one of the men said, as they moved out the door.

"He will receive proper instruction and care—here at home," Stephen said, and his voice was strained, as though his teeth were clenched.

Mother's head was down, and she never looked up at any of us as they led her away.

"What will happen to her?" Martina asked through tears.

"We can only pray she won't lose faith while they keep her in the Institute," Stephen whispered.

Suddenly my voice returned and I heard myself sobbing, "Why are they taking Mother away?"

"They say she's sick," Stephen whispered to me. "They say they'll make her well again."

"How long will she be gone? Will she be gone forever, too—like Father?"

"I don't think so, Jael," he said, and I saw him try to smile.

That night when the windows were shuttered as usual, Stephen read these words to us from The Book, "Dear friends, do not be surprised at the painful trial you are suffering, as though something strange were happening to you. But commit yourselves to God and continue to do good."

"What good will that do?" Darien mumbled. "They'll just keep working on us, slowly chipping away until they can catch each of us weak and vulnerable—like they did with Mother. They've gotten her in their snares now, and there's nothing we can do."

Stephen closed the thick book and took a deep breath. "Darien, please. Why must you always be on the verge of an explosion?"

"What do you want, Stephen? Some totally disciplined mind like the Council teaches?"

Stephen didn't answer, but turned to look at me. "We need to be strong—and, yes, even think rationally, for Jael's sake."

"Think rationally?" Martina asked. "That's what they keep feeding us at school. Are you giving in to their System, Stephen?"

"No, I just mean Darien is right. They'll keep working to draw us away until we're each alone. I'm not sure we can keep on fighting them forever. But we need to remember our strength is in our family, in each other. We must always cling to that." Stephen's eyes seemed to bore into mine as he continued speaking. "Why do you think they chose Father for the most dangerous missions in the war? Why do you think they sent the Questioner to Mother on a day when she was alone and weak? They *will* keep looking for each of our weak points. That's why we have to keep being strong together."

Now he was looking at Darien.

"What have we ever done to any of them?" Darien asked.

"Nothing but try to be ourselves," Stephen replied. "It's just that here on Terres, people fear old ways like ours. They want to be told what to think, so they let the Council control them. They're afraid of those of us who don't want to be controlled, who try to think for ourselves."

I was watching the light in his eyes glow and fade as he spoke.

"I know you don't understand all this now, Jael," he said. "But I hope someday you'll remember these words and know what they mean." Then he turned to Darien and Martina. "Jael is the one they want, I think. That's why they targeted his parents first. They didn't think we could fill their shoes. It won't be easy, but we must teach Jael as we were taught by our parents—so he, too, can choose for himself when the time comes."

"That's okay for you to say, Stephen." Darien said angrily. "You're out of school, and don't get fed their stuff day after day. It's driving *me* crazy!"

"Yeah," Martina added. "Sometimes I think it would be easier to just accept what they say and avoid the problems."

"Do not be surprised at the painful trial…" Stephen repeated softly. "It seems it's always been hard for the King's people to face the world and its ways. But we mustn't give up just because something is hard. Remember Father and Mother—and do it for them—and Jael." Then his voice tapered off and disappeared into silence.

"All right," Darien said at last. "But what do we do now? Who can support us?"

"I've reached my Journeyman level in Star Corps," said Stephen. "Soon I'll be on the Space Shuttle. I can earn enough credits to support us."

"And I can look after the house and garden," said Martina.

"But you still need to go to school," Stephen said.

"Why?"

"To keep greater suspicion from falling on us."

"Oh, all right. But who will watch Jael during the days?"

"What about Anha?" Darien asked. "Mother spoke well of her."

"Yes, I know how to reach her," said Stephen. "Do you think she can be trusted?"

"Mother thought so," Darien said.

"Okay. I'll talk to her tomorrow."

So, then it was just the four of us, and Stephen did his best to keep us feeling like a family. He began to ride me on his shoulders around the house, and get us into tickle games on the floor, where we laughed until we ached. Martina would smile at us from her work in the galley or the garden room.

She let me help her, too. I learned how to tell which red and gold fruits were ripe for picking, and to clean and cook the fresh-smelling green and orange vegetables. She also showed me how to test the liquid solutions and add the colored powders that made the plants grow well. I watched carefully as she pruned and trimmed the plants for better fruit. The warm-smelling garden room became my favorite place to be.

Sometimes while she was working, she'd tell me stories. My favorites were about Earth, the place Mother had mentioned, somewhere far away across vast distances of space.

"Our ancestors came from there," she said. "Now that we've been on Terres for so long, the Council wants us to believe Earth is a myth, and only The System matters. But Father always told me not to believe that. We must *not* forget the past but learn from it," she added. "The Council wants us to believe Terres-City is the only inhabitable part of this planet. But I believe there are places beyond the Peaks and in the Wilds where other people can live. Maybe in those places the people are free to believe as they choose, the way Father taught us we should."

I loved to hear these stories about strange and faraway places. I'd try to imagine what they looked like. But when I finally did see some of these places, later in my life, they weren't at all like I'd imagined them.

One day she added, "Father said we must think for ourselves because that's a gift God gave us."

"Who is God?" I asked. "How can we find out, if we can't see him?"

She was silent for a long time. "You know, Jael, I'm not sure myself. Father probably wanted to tell us much more as we grew older, but he never got the chance."

"And now Mother won't get to either, I bet."

She looked into my eyes and said, "I hope she'll be

back soon. Meanwhile, your brothers and I will just have to do the best we can."

After that I didn't ask questions so much. I didn't like to see her shake her head and say, "I don't know," or "I'm not sure."

Darien didn't smile much after Mother was gone. He spent most of his time in his sleeping room, playing music on a stringed instrument he called a manitar. Sometimes, Martina would join him, playing her flute. He often sang with his eyes closed as though he could see the music that way. He didn't mind if I listened, but he didn't like me to talk to him. So, I just sat and watched his fingers fly over the strings as the music floated into the air around us.

I began to see how Darien was very different from Stephen in many ways. Their personalities were as different as the color of their hair. Darien's was straight and dark, while Stephen's was blond and full of curls. Stephen was older and taller, but their eyes were alike—a deep green that seemed to look right through you. You could tell from their faces they were brothers, but Darien was more brooding, dark like his hair. He didn't make people around him feel better the way Stephen did. I guess I looked like them, too, but my hair was blond and wavy, and I wondered which one's personality I would follow.

Martina looked a lot like Darien, except she was a girl, so her dark hair hung long and straight when she let down the clasps that held it up when she was working. I liked the way she shook it out and let the strands fly when she did this. But I think I remember her eyes the most. They were a soft, rich green, and they shone whenever she smiled.

Both she and Darien had round faces and smooth cheeks, but Stephen and I had more angular features, with cheeks that looked hollower. Sometimes I'd stand at the looking glass and puff air into my cheeks to see if I could look more like Martina. And I'd stare a long time trying to see what color my eyes were. Some days they seemed to be dull grey, and other days they were almost the green of Martina's, but paler.

I looked up to Stephen a great deal, and thought he looked so brave and dashing in his sky-blue Star Corps uniform. I loved to sit beside him while he showed me pictures of the various space craft and the orbiting space stations and outposts of our planet and its moons. Every night, I looked out my window at the stars, dreaming of voyaging out there with Stephen.

I probably asked him the same question every day, "Can I go with you on a voyage sometime? At least to Luna One, please?"

He'd laugh and sometimes rumple my hair. "When you get older, perhaps. It's not easy to get a ride on a rocket. You have to be cleared."

"Cleared?" I asked. "How do I do that, with soap?"

Martina laughed then. "If it takes soap, you'll be out of luck, the little you ever use."

When it was the three of us like this, we could almost forget the empty space we each had in our heart. But when Darien was home, things were usually much quieter. If we laughed too loud, he'd stomp out of the room. He never talked very much, and it was hard to know what to say when he was around. We were almost glad, though ashamed to admit it, when he got a job playing his manitar at a nearby club most evenings.

Martina and Stephen were teaching me to read by this time, but I surprised them with how many of the books on our shelves I could read already.

"Isn't it amazing how well Jael can read?" Martina told Stephen one day.

"I'm sure it means something," he nodded. "Especially since most adults don't even bother to read anymore."

"Why is that?" I asked.

"Well, with the new Terminals the Council has installed in people's homes, all they need to do is listen while someone else reads to them," he said.

"But why don't we have a Terminal?"

Stephen looked up suddenly at my question. "Father thought it let the Council have too much power," he said. "After all, if you can read the books yourself, *you* can decide what they mean. If the Terminal reads it for you, the Council gets to decide what it will and will not say. They can even change the words to suit themselves."

Once Stephen brought home drawings of his space shuttle. He showed me diagrams and maps of his flights back and forth to the space stations and moons. I was fascinated these things existed in a realm I couldn't see. Stephen would always smile and try to answer all the many questions I asked.

"This is all so amazing," I said. "I wish I could see it with my own eyes."

"Someday perhaps you'll get to voyage in space. Then you can see it all for yourself."

"You mean I can join the Star Corps?" I asked excitedly. Of course, I wanted to be just like my big brother when I grew up.

"No, I'm afraid not. Only firstborn can join the Star Corps."

"But why? Is that the Council's law?"

"No," he said gently. "It's because only firstborn can cross the GAP. But there are other ways to get into space."

I used to sit and think a lot about these things, looking at all the pictures and gazing out my window at the stars. One night, Stephen saw me looking at the sky as he was heading to his own bedroom.

"Beautiful, isn't it?" he whispered.

"Yes," I nodded. "I just feel like I belong out there."

"Perhaps you do," he said.

There was a rustling sound as he pulled something out of his pocket. It was a frayed, wrinkled piece of paper with his handwriting on it.

"Here," he smiled. "This is for you. It's something I found in The Book a long time ago. I've always felt it was special to me, but now it should be yours. Can you read it?"

I nodded and read the words softly, " 'The heavens declare the glory of God, and the firmament shows the work of his hands.' Wow! But this is yours, I shouldn't take it."

He closed my hand over the piece of paper and whispered. "I want you to have it. I know you'll treasure it as much as I have. Keep it safe."

CHAPTER 6

GLIMPSE OF HEAVEN

One day Stephen came home with a big smile on his face.

"What's up with you?" Martina asked from the galley.

"I managed to get it!" he said, great excitement in his voice.

"Get what?" I chimed in, from where I was helping prepare some vegetables for supper.

"Permission to take you guys on a short shuttle flight," he smiled.

"All of us?" Martina cried, clapping her hands. Flour from the bread she was kneading flew all around her face.

"Well, you and Jael," said Stephen. "Darien will be at his music job."

I didn't admit it, but I was glad of this. Stephen and Martina were the ones who talked to me and played with me the most. Darien always seemed to be sad or angry and hardly ever talked to any of us anymore.

"When do we go?" I asked.

"Day after tomorrow."

I was so excited, I could hardly wait for the time to pass. The day we were to report to the Space Port, Martina didn't have school. Darien went out to get ready for his music job. Stephen helped me get into the suit he'd brought. Martina already had hers on, since she put it on when she got up. I could tell she was as excited as I was.

Soon, the three of us were walking to the Tube station down our street, another first for me. We sat in one corner of a long, narrow car with seats in groups of four all along both sides. There were soft blue cushions on them, which gave around my backside as I sat down.

There wasn't much sound as the car started to move. Stephen told me there were several cars hooked together, but we couldn't really see them. There was a glimpse of the one in front of ours through the sliding door near our seats. The doors gave a hissing sound each time they opened and closed.

Most of what we could see outside the small windows of our car went by so fast I could barely make out the buildings and towers. Then we entered a tunnel and every-thing outside went black.

"We're underground now, Jael," Martina said. She was used to taking the Tube to school.

The car seemed to be gliding very fast. Once in awhile there was a slight shifting that moved it side to side.

"That's where we're changing tracks," said Stephen.

I just kept my nose closely pressed to the window, watching and waiting, even when there was nothing but black to see. Then suddenly, light flashed in my eyes. We were back above ground. I could see groundcars going by on a street, and they seemed to be crawling because we were going so much faster.

"Wow!" I exclaimed, "It feels like we're flying."

"Wait until we get on the Shuttle," laughed Stephen.

Just at that moment, the car around us shuddered, and a strange loud roaring filled our ears. Outside the window, there was a flash of color and then a dark blur.

"What was that?" I cried.

"We just met another train going the other way," Martina told me.

"It sure was going fast," I marveled.

"So are we," Stephen smiled.

Then we could feel the train slowing down as it came to the Spaceport station, and people began to get out of their seats and line up by the doors. Stephen helped me get up and join the nearest line, with Martina behind me. The door in front of us hissed and opened, and we stepped out onto the platform into a big crowd of people, all walking toward large doors ahead of us.

"Stay close to me, Jael," warned Stephen. "You too, Martina."

We kept walking for what seemed a long time, past

shop stalls where people were selling food, snacks and trinkets. Stephen didn't stop, however, until he came to a set of double doors which said, "Restricted Entry." Here he flashed a card through a little box, and the doors opened.

"Welcome, Stephen," said a voice, but it must have been a recording of some kind, because I couldn't see anyone.

"That's the computer's recognition program," Stephen explained. "I've already put you two into the system, so they know you're with me."

There were only a few chairs in this area, and Stephen walked past them all. Ahead there was a console with a glass screen standing on it. When he touched it, pictures appeared where there was nothing but clear glass before.

"What's that?" I asked in wonder.

"It's a Terminal," Martina said.

"Does it know who you are, Stephen?"

"Sure does, Jael."

With his finger, he moved some of the pictures around on the screen. When I looked again, there were pictures of the three of us together.

"Where did those pictures came from?" Martina asked.

"The computer just took them," Stephen replied.

The next thing he did was move each picture with his finger until they were inside the outline of a Shuttle.

"Okay, we're cleared to go," he smiled.

"And luckily, no soap needed!" laughed Martina.

Just then, another door opened beyond the desk with the Terminal. As we stepped inside, the doors closed quickly behind us. After walking down a short tunnel, we entered a small room. Here Stephen adjusted our suits and his, and pulled helmets over our heads.

"We need air helmets on this flight," he explained. "We'll be going high enough to be out of breathable atmosphere."

I wasn't completely sure what this meant, but I thought we looked funny. "We look like we have bubble-heads!" I laughed.

Next, we went through a door on the other side of the little room. It was almost like we were back in the train. There were rows of soft seats here, too. But there weren't as many, and these had sky-blue fabric on them, a perfect match to Stephen's uniform. The windows here were smaller, and the plastiglas was much thicker.

Stephen helped me get strapped into my seat, while Martina worked at getting her straps done herself.

"Good job, Sis!" said Stephen. "You'd think you were an old pro at this."

She smiled back at him.

Finally, we were ready. Numbers flashed on the screen in front of the seats, counting backwards to zero. Then came a shuddering sound and a feeling like someone was sitting on my chest.

"I can hardly breathe," cried Martina.

"Just take long slow breaths," Stephen assured us. "The G-force will be over soon."

I was surprised they could even talk, for I didn't have enough breath left for that. But Stephen was right. Soon the pressure was gone, and I felt very light-headed. Stephen undid his straps and floated up in front of me.

"Weightless time!" he laughed. "Come on, it's actually fun."

Soon all three of us were drifting around the cabin with others who were there. At the windows, we could look out and see a marvelous sight.

The sky was black, and here and there were lights that burned with an uncanny glow. "Those are stars," Stephen told me, and pointed to some he could name.

Then a large brown and green orb came into sight, filling half the sky before us. "There's home, Terres," Martina whispered. "It sure looks different from up here."

"Can you see where the City is, Jael?" Stephen asked.

"Is it that brownish area?"

"You got it!" he laughed.

Then we just floated and looked in silence for awhile.

"Stephen," I whispered at last, "This reminds me of that verse on the paper you gave me: 'The heavens declare the glory of God'…"

"Sure does," he nodded.

"Is this what Heaven looks like?" Martina asked.

"Could be," he smiled. "No one really knows what Heaven is like."

"I bet it's something like this," I sighed. "I wish we could stay here forever."

"Sorry we can't this time," said Stephen, patting me on the back. The motion sent me into a slow spin.

"Someday we'll all be together in Heaven, though," said Martina, "Even Mother and Father will be there with us."

I closed my eyes for a moment, trying to imagine what they would look like, our whole family together. 'Yes, that would be heavenly,' I thought.

This was what I kept in my mind as we traveled back home, first in the Shuttle, then in the Tube. It had been a truly amazing day.

["Wow, that must have been awesome!" said Danny.

"It really was," Jael nodded.

"I sure wish we could go into space someday," Ginna sighed.

"Perhaps you will," said Jon.

"I don't see how," she shrugged. "Only astronauts and scientists get to go from here on Earth."

"Still, you never know what the future may hold," Jon said.]

CHAPTER 7

THE WILDS
AND THE UNDERGROUND

Martina and Darien were still in school then, though Darien was almost finished. I wasn't old enough for school yet, and since Martina taught me to read and write, I wasn't sure if I'd go to school like the others. She said I already knew more than they could teach me in school, because they used only the Terminal there, no books.

When everyone was gone during the day, I was taken to stay with the woman Anha, who lived close by. There was a girl there just my age named Raina. She had soft reddish-brown hair and brown eyes that seemed to shine like gold. I liked playing games with her indoors at Anha's house, but I liked it even more when we could go outdoors and run around in the play area beside the house.

Raina had an older brother named Jason. Whenever he came to get her after school, I'd watch him in fascination. I'd never seen hair like his before. It was red and shining, and when the light outside shone on it, there were bright flecks of gold. He and Raina both had brown dots all over their noses and cheeks. She called them 'freckles.' Once she even let me touch them, but they just felt like the rest of her skin.

One day, Martina came for me at the same time as Jason. When they started talking to each other, Martina seemed to act strangely. Her eyes were shining, but her cheeks were red, and she kept looking down at her feet. But she was smiling, so I decided perhaps she liked Jason.

After that, Jason and Martina almost always came together to get us. Once when I was looking out, I saw them coming far down the street. Jason was holding her hand, but he let go when they got close to Anha's house. I didn't ask Martina anything about it, but I liked it when the four of us began going places together. I was glad to be with Raina more.

My favorite outing was going to Neptune Spire, the tallest building in Terres-City. We'd go underground in the Tube. When it stopped we climbed back above ground into the midst of many tall buildings, all with smooth sides gleaming in the sun. Through the busy streets we moved into a lush green place called a 'park'. This was one of the few places in the City where I saw plants growing in the open air instead of in the glass garden-houses. The smells and sights overwhelmed me. It was so much bigger than the garden room we had, or even the one at Anha's. On some days, the air stirred the leaves above us, and we could feel it brush gently against our faces.

Neptune Spire was in the center of the park, so tall it seemed to reach all the way to the sky. I craned my neck to look, trying to see exactly where the top was. Some days, the shining top seemed to wink down at us in the rays of Regelian, but other times the sides of the spire really would disappear into the clouds. On those cloudy days, all we would see when we rode to the top was the swirling grays, blues, and whites of those clouds below us.

But the bright sunny days were the best. Then we could almost see forever when we looked out the tall windows at the top of the spire. Below us was Terres-City with bright bubbles of shining colored glass on the building tops. If we strained our eyes and looked as far as we could into the distance, we saw a vast green expanse to the east of the city. Farther to the east, on the clearest of days, we'd catch a glimpse of jagged peaks emerging from the shimmering haze. They hardly looked real, but more like something painted on the sky far off at the edge of the world.

["Peaks at the edge of the world!" Danny gasped. "Just like ours here."

Jael smiled and nodded to him. "This is only the beginning of parallels, Daniel."]

One day when we were on the spire, I asked Martina, "What's out there at the edge of the world?"

"The Wilds are," she said.

"Doesn't anyone live there?" Raina asked.

"Just the Redlarks," Jason shrugged.

"What are the Redlarks?" Raina pressed.

"They're people who like to live in the Wilds, Sis," said Jason softly.

"But why don't they live in the City?" Raina persisted. "How can they get food or anything way out there?"

I was as curious as Raina, but then Martina said tensely, "We shouldn't talk about this here in public."

"Why should you care?" snapped Jason. "They're just renegades who deserve the punishment they get."

"No one deserves to be declared non-existent," she retorted.

Jason's ears were getting red, a sign he was really angry. "Look, kids, we'd better talk about this some other time."

He reached to take Martina's hand, but she pulled away, stalking to the other side of the viewing room.

When I looked at Raina, I could see she was just as confused as I was. I shrugged at her and turned back to look toward the east again. My eyes couldn't seem to leave those peaks, shimmering so far away.

I was happy when we spent these days together, when I could walk down the street holding Raina's hand while Jason held my sister's. I remember the first time I saw him put his arm around Martina. He pulled back when he saw me looking. Soon, however, he began to leave it there around her waist and give me a wink when I saw him. When I tried hard to wink back, both my eyes always closed together.

Jason started to take her out in the evenings, too. She'd always spend lots of time in front of the mirror getting ready and trying to decide what to wear. I teased her about it, but she only laughed, "I like to look extra nice for Jason. After all, I want him to be proud of me, don't I?"

One night, I stayed up late reading and was still awake when they came in. Quickly, I turned out the light, expecting Martina to come up the spiral staircase at any moment. But there was only silence. Then I heard a soft sound like a sigh.

Creeping very slowly to the staircase, I peeked over and there in a patch of moonlight I could see him holding her very close in his arms, their lips pressed together. They seemed to be enjoying themselves. Then she laid her head on his shoulder, and he gently stroked her hair. The moonlight was dancing in his red hair. Then he began to nuzzle her under the chin and kiss her neck, and she sighed again. I felt I was intruding by watching, but I was frozen to the spot and couldn't move a muscle.

Finally, they parted slowly.

"I'd better go," he whispered.

"See you soon?"

"Yes, Martina, as soon as possible."

He kissed her again very quickly, then slipped out the door.

I flew back to my bed and threw the covers over my head. But it was a long time before I heard her quiet footfalls on the stairs.

A few days later, Raina and I got to play outside and build one of our imaginary houses. We usually played Star Corps, pretending to voyage to strange and distant worlds. But this day we decided to play 'parents' as Raina called it. I was the father and when I came home from work she would fix our pretend supper. Then, since she said we must be fair, we'd trade places.

"Honey," I'd say, like she had, "How was your day?"

"Oh just fine, darling," she replied. "Say Jael-"

"What?"

"Maybe we should try to do like real grownups do."

"Aren't we already?" I'd never seen my father when he came home to Mother, because he'd been gone to the wars before I could even walk or talk.

"Well, almost. But when you or I come home, we should kiss," she said.

"You mean put our lips together?"

"Sure, let's try."

"Oh, let's just kiss on the cheek," I said. "That's what my brothers and sister do."

"Come on, Jael."

"Oh, okay." I closed my eyes and puckered.

I pressed my lips against hers, but they just felt hard, cold and wet. When I pulled back, her eyes were still squinched shut.

"You can open your eyes, silly." I said. "What was so special about that?"

"I don't know," she shrugged. "Grownups seem to like it. And Jason and Martina sure do."

"Have you seen them, too?" I asked.

"Sure. What do you think it means?"

"I don't know. Kissing doesn't seem like such a big deal to me."

"Me neither."

Then she went and got the pretend tray of food she fixed for our dinner. "Do you really grow your own food?" she asked suddenly. "In dirt and chemicals? Why don't you just go to the markets like we do?"

"I don't know. Martina says her cooking tastes better. Our mother always cooked for us, so Martina does, too. And I like to stand in the garden-room with all the growing things. It smells so good and fresh in there, like the park."

"Well I guess it is nice. I like the one here at Anha's. I'd never seen one before I came here. It seems like a lot more work to make all those meals yourself, though."

"Anha does, too," I said.

"But you have to help her."

"I like to help. It's fun, especially with Martina."

"You know Jason says your family is really different," Raina said suddenly. "Is it true you can really read words on paper?"

"Sure, that's fun, too."

"But why bother? You can get everything you need from a Terminal. Why read myths in a bunch of old books? That seems like a waste of time."

"Well, I *like* to read!" I retorted. Then I wondered why her questions made me anxious. Something in the tone of her voice made me uneasy. I wondered for a moment if perhaps I should read her one of the stories I'd found, to help her see it was okay to be different. But then I decided this probably wouldn't change her mind. We didn't talk about the books for a long time after that.

Later that day, I was listening to Darien play his manitar after we ate supper. He must have been in a better mood that evening because he was singing words from a song he'd found in one of our old books:

"Alas my love you do me wrong,
To cast me off so discourteously;
When I have loved you for so long,
Delighting in your company."

"What does that mean?" I asked.

"Oh, it's an old song about a lady named Greensleeves."

"That's a strange name," I said.

"Well, maybe she liked green clothes," he shrugged. "Anyway, some guy is in love with her, but she doesn't seem to care for him." He was gazing out the window with a faraway look in his eyes.

"Do you think Jason and Martina are in love?" I asked.

Suddenly he was staring hard at me, fire in his eyes. "What makes you say that?" he demanded.

"Well, I've seen them kissing. Raina says that's what grownups do."

Then he grabbed my arm and squeezed it much too hard. "They're too young!" Suddenly, he stormed out of the room, leaving me breathless and confused.

Soon I heard him downstairs talking to Stephen, their voices so loud I could hear them without even going onto the staircase.

"She's too young to be carrying on like that with him!" Darien was shouting. "You know as well as I do where this will lead. He'll have her in the Underground before we know it!"

"Martina is old enough to take care of her own choices and her own emotions," said Stephen. His voice sounded even and calm, but I could hear the tension underneath.

"She is not!" Darien retorted. "She's younger than I am!"

"Look, Darien, just because you think you can hide from the world and refuse to share yourself with anyone doesn't mean we all have to. Just because you're afraid."

"You shut up! Father wouldn't approve of it either, and you know it."

Stephen's voice grew suddenly louder now. "You need to stop this, Darien. What makes you so sure what Father would've done? And just because you want to retreat into yourself for the rest of your life, that's no reason to expect the rest of us to. Father taught us to treasure freedom, not coercion."

"You're the one who's weakening," Darien cried. "Father taught us to stand up for Truth and for what we believe in. Martina is heading for trouble and you just want to stand by and watch."

Then the door slammed, and Darien was gone into the night.

I wasn't sure whether I should go down to Stephen or not, so I sat at the top of the staircase for a long time. Darkness gradually settled across the room, and still Stephen sat on the floor cushion with his head in his hands. Then the outside door opened, and two figures stepped in, Jason and Martina. He was holding her close and soon was kissing her. There was a rustling sound as he moved his hands in her tunic.

"Not here!" she whispered sharply. "My brothers will hear you."

"What does that matter?" His voice was very deep.

"With my brothers, it matters a lot."

"Oh, all right."

A little space of light appeared between them.

"I guess I'd better go. I'll see you tomorrow." His voice seemed filled with disappointment.

The door closed softly, and she turned toward the staircase. Then she let out a sharp cry.

"Stephen, you scared me! We didn't mean-"

"Didn't mean for me to see you? I'm sure of *that*."

"We weren't going to do anything."

"Hey, it's all right 'Tina." His voice was gentler now. "Would you like to talk a while, like we used to when you were younger?"

She nodded silently and joined him on the cushion.

"Do you feel special about Jason?"

"Well, in some ways, yes. He's nice to be with, though sometimes we argue. He doesn't understand our ways and thinks we're being rebellious with our old books and all."

'I wondered about that,' I thought to myself, hanging on every word.

"But when he kisses me," she went on, "I get strange feelings inside—all warm and, well—excited."

"I can understand that." There was a smile in Stephen's voice.

"Who have you been kissing, big brother?" she teased.

He just chuckled and refused to answer.

After a long silence, Martina asked, "Stephen, what's the Underground?"

"Hasn't Jason told you?"

"Oh, he hints about it a lot. But I wanted to know what you think."

Again, the silence came. Then I heard him take a deep breath that was almost a sigh. "You know, of course, the Council and the Masters tell us we must have disciplined minds, controlling our passions and avoiding emotion, and that we must seek the highest reason and logic."

"Yeah, they keep telling us all that in school."

"But you also know Father taught us the body is not evil altogether, and to just deny your body is not the answer. He tried to teach us to seek a balance somehow. But I don't think the Council agrees."

"I know," she said. "But where does the Underground fit?"

"Well, it's hard to explain, but I'll try," he sighed. "The Underground is a place where people of Terres go when their mind can no longer control their body. It's a place they think they hide from the Council and the System to be released for awhile. But I think the Council is really behind the Underground, because they use it as another way to control people."

"They just pretend they don't know about it?" she asked.

"Yeah, I guess that's it. It's sort of like when you try to

fool yourself. Father used to say it was like 'the right hand not knowing what the left hand was doing'."

"That's silly, Stephen."

"Well I guess. But the Underground is not silly. It goes to the opposite extreme and denies the mind altogether. It's a place of unleashed passions, and, in the end, of pain."

Martina didn't reply this time. The darkness seemed to deepen around them, and it was a long time before she spoke again.

"Sometimes I think I'm looking for something Jason doesn't even know exists, something I find only in books and in our home."

"You mean love?"

"Yeah."

"Well, if you aren't sure about Jason—he does come from the System, so it's probably impossible for him to understand."

"I don't know what to think. I feel good with him in a way I don't anywhere else. I feel like I could fly, and the pleasure goes deep inside me. It makes me wonder what the Underground *is* like. Jason tells me it's like our kissing, only more."

"You know, there's a strange thing about physical contact," Stephen said. "Lots of times it can feel like love when it's just—well, something called lust. Sometimes someone kisses you and it doesn't really matter who it is, it just feels good. But that doesn't necessarily mean it's love."

"You sound like you've had lots of experience," she said.

"Well I am a few years older than you, and out of the control of school." I could hear a slight smile in his voice. "What I'm trying to say, 'Tina, is be careful. When it's love, you'll feel good with the person in all kinds of ways and places, not just when he kisses you. The Underground isn't like this. It's a place of secrets, where things happen people would be ashamed of in the light of day."

"That sure doesn't sound like what Jason tells me."

"Jason may be deceived, or he may know the truth and choose not to tell you. Please beware of people like that."

As silence settled again, I could hear them breathing. I tried to hold my breath, hoping they couldn't hear me. Just as she got up to go, Stephen spoke again, this time very softly, "Just remember, if anything should happen to me-"

"Why should anything happen to you?" There was a sudden tone of fear in her voice, and I felt it, too. Hadn't we lost enough already, with both parents gone?

"If it should, please try to keep on teaching Jael what Mother and Father taught us."

"I'll do my best, big brother. But you'd better not let anything happen to you, just the same."

CHAPTER 8

NOTHING BUT DUST

I know Stephen tried to be there for us, but some things just happen, and there seems to be no reason or logic to it. Even though the Council of Terres kept telling us reason was the highest of goods. And so, a morning came that still stands out sharp and clear in my mind—so sharp and clear it still hurts.

I could see the light of our sun shining into the room, the plastiglas of the window glowing orange, a reflection of the brightness promising a new day. But this day didn't dawn with any joy or hope.

Darien sat on the floor with his manitar in his hands hanging still, the instrument silent. Martina sat on a large cushion, holding me in her lap. I could feel the stiffness of her body, and it made me uncomfortable, but I didn't try to move away from her.

"Martina, Darien, Jael, I know this is very difficult for you. It's also hard for me, but I wanted to tell you myself."

A man in a sky-blue Star Corps uniform was speaking, his voice very low. A ray of sunlight caught the captain's emblem on his shoulder, and it flashed in my eyes.

"Tell us all of it," said Darien, his voice like ice. "We want to know everything, Captain."

The captain didn't seem to want to look at Darien, and Martina's eyes were riveted to the floor. His eyes searched for someone to look at, and came to rest on me. I tried to look back, but couldn't see much for my tears.

"Your brother was a very good man," he said. "In fact, he was one of our most promising recruits. He seemed to have a greater-than-normal measure of the power of the firstborn, the GAP-crossers."

"Spare us the pretty words and get on with it." Darien snapped.

"Darien!" Martina spoke for the first time since the captain arrived. "Stop now. You're just making it harder for all of us, including the captain."

"Darien, I'm sorry, too," said the captain evenly. "It's my loss as well. Stephen was my best friend."

"Just tell us how he died."

I could hear the great pain in Darien's voice and wanted to do something for him, young as I was. Quickly, I slipped from Martina's lap and moved to his side.

"Darien, I know I'm just a little brother, but I love you." Tears were blinding my eyes again.

He raised his hand, and for an instant I thought he might strike me. But then his hand dropped and slowly reached to my cheeks and brushed the tears away.

"You're lucky," he said gruffly, "You're still young enough to cry."

"I'll cry *for* you, if that's all I can do to help," I said.

"Thanks, Jael," he whispered, setting aside his manitar and pulling me onto his lap. I couldn't remember the last time he'd done this, so I leaned into his embrace, trying to help us both feel better.

The captain sat quietly through all this, and Martina went back to staring at the floor. After silence settled, in which all I could hear was Darien's breathing, he began again:

"It was just a routine shuttle flight to Space Station Alpha. On re-entry, the shuttle lost transceiver contact. We tried to track, but the sensors couldn't find him. We even tried to override the automatic pilot, but nothing worked. When we found the remains of the shuttle, everything was burned up, even the flight recorder. Stephen had gotten under his fire shield, as we're always taught. That's where we found him."

"If he was under the shield and he wasn't burned, how did he die?" Darien snapped. "Don't those shields do their job?"

"Oh, they work," the captain replied coolly. "I owe

my own life to one. But everything has limits. The fire must have been super-hot, and seared his lungs. His body didn't burn, but still he was dead."

"His body survived, but he didn't?" Darien said.

I was puzzled at these words. How could Stephen still have a body if he was dead?

The captain's voice continued behind my thoughts, "There will have to be a complete investigation, of course."

"Of course," Darien echoed. "What does that matter now? Stephen is dead, and no investigation will bring him back."

This was more than Martina could take. With a stifled cry, she ran up the spiral staircase. Soon we could hear her sobbing in her room.

The captain rose to leave. Just as he reached the door, he turned and looked back at us. "Just one word of advice, Darien," he said. "Be careful about what you say to the officials. Your anger could be a threat to all of you. And as you said, it won't bring Stephen back, anyway."

Tears began streaming down my cheeks again, and I was in the midst of a great sob, for my breath had left me. 'What does any of this mean?' I wondered. 'Why do all these things keep happening to us?'

Darien's face was still red with anger after the captain left.

***

In the following days, I'd see that anger in him often. But there was something else in Darien now, as though a battle was raging inside him. He tried to remain quiet and strong on the outside, but I could sense his aching pain. I wondered if it would help him to cry, but he never did that I saw, though Martina and I did often.

As days passed, many Council and Star Corps officials came and went. From the top of the staircase, I was witness to many loud arguments Martina and Darien had with them. Though not all of it made sense to me, I began to see more clearly how our family's beliefs were in conflict with the Terres Council.

Time after time, uniformed officials came, telling us what we were required to do with Stephen's body. As they talked, their eyes would keep roving to the shelves of books around the room, and they seemed to stare a lot at our garden-room. None ever said a word about them, however. Instead they concentrated on the subject of Stephen's cremation. Their words still echo in my mind:

"Cremation is the only proper way to dispose of a body. It's the way of logic and enlightenment, for we know the body is wholly unclean and evil. Only the mind and soul are good; only the mind is capable of rising to higher levels. And this can't happen until the body is finally destroyed. The body is nothing but dust, and the sooner it returns to dust, the sooner it can release the mind to be pure and free of evil."

So the officials' words went, day after day. And the words Darien replied with are also still clear in my mind:

"Where is it recorded, except by the Council, that the mind and body must be separated? In life, they move and breathe together—one cannot exist without the other. To be fully himself, a person needs both. You and your System try to separate body and mind by force. But this just results in torn and separated lives—a calm face for the day, and the blind passion of the Underground by night. Stephen was admired and unique because he wasn't half a man, like those who live these falsely separated System lives."

["Jael, how can you remember all this?" Jon interrupted. "You were so young."

"I'm not sure, but somehow it's seared in my mind. Maybe it was the trauma, or perhaps Martina told me more when I was older. It's all in here, though." He took a deep breath as he tapped his forehead. Then he continued:]

Martina found an old book describing an ancient custom of preserving the dead body and burying it in the ground.

"See, it's a sign that Stephen's body was preserved in the crash," she said. "What's wrong with keeping the memory of the whole person and not destroying the body?"

The longer she argued with the System officials, the

more obsessed Martina became with this idea. I couldn't see it made much difference. Stephen was dead, and I was old enough to understand we'd never see him again, just like Father.

Martina and Darien talked of these things late into the nights, as I lay on my bed listening and trying to understand. Perhaps it *was* important to keep Stephen's body whole, as a way to keep his memory more intact. I remembered what Stephen had told Martina about the Underground, and how the mind and body were supposed to work in balance together, not be forcibly separated.

My sleep was very fitful, haunted by dreams of bodies floating in air and water, looking for their minds. Each morning, I lay listless in the hot, damp sheets. Martina often came and put a cool cloth on my forehead, smiling wanly.

I don't know if I was sick or just exhausted, but the results were the same. For many days, I was too weak to get out of bed. Martina finally began to worry about me more than she did about the burial arguments. Meanwhile, the officials kept coming a few at a time each day. We didn't worry about how much of our house they were seeing, but perhaps we should have.

One morning, when I finally had a peaceful night, Martina took me to see Stephen's body. It seemed they'd found a way to preserve it while the arguments continued, and Martina took this as a hopeful sign.

He was lying on a piece of smooth, stony material. Both the body and its bed looked very cold, like the bare room they were in. I looked for a long time. His strong arms now looked weak and limp; his face seemed sunken, and there was a strangeness about it. It looked somewhat like my older brother, but something was missing. His eyes were closed, and somehow I knew they'd never shine and sparkle again. Where was his mind and soul? I began to wonder if the officials were right and this body *was* nothing but dust. The real Stephen seemed to be gone. Where was he?

But how could this be? My mind ached from trying to understand. How could he be gone and still lying here, too? My throat closed painfully so I couldn't even ask Martina any questions. I hardly even remember her leading me out of that room and taking me home.

In the end the Council won, of course. After all, they had the strength of a planet behind them, and we were only children. Martina insisted on putting the cremation ashes in an urn. The Council said we should scatter the ashes so they could return to the dust they came from, but still Martina refused. Instead, she set the urn on a little table in our house, beside the west window where the morning sun would catch it, making it glow like brass.

"This way, he can watch the sunrise," she said.

I wondered if she really meant this. It sounded crazy to me.

"Stephen is still with us this way," she said. "This is all we have left of him now, but we won't part with it. The Council thinks they've beaten us, but we're still together as long as we have his ashes here. We'll keep him. He belongs to us, and we won't give him up."

CHAPTER 9

FAREWELLS NEVER END

Time passed then, though I'm not sure how long. I was still young and the days seemed to melt together. Looking back now, certain moments stand out stark and clear, like peaks above a dense fog. But down in the fog things are obscure to me.

I do remember that a silence came over our house again. The place was even more full of tension than when Mother was taken. I began to realize Stephen was the one who'd talked to me and played with me the most. Now I was more alone than I'd ever been before. Sometimes, I woke at night to hear someone screaming, only to find it was me. The first few times Darien came to me. I knew he was trying to take Stephen's place, but it was very hard for him.

One night I seemed unable to control the cries coming from me. They were welling up so deep inside they seemed to come from someone else. In my dream, I'd been slowly falling apart into sparkling dust. When I finally became aware of myself, Darien was shaking me. I could hear shouting but the words made no sense. Then I felt pain in my cheeks, as if someone was slapping me.

Then I heard Martina's voice like a distant bell, "Stop it! You're hurting him."

"He won't stop," Darien cried. "He won't listen to reason."

"Reason! You sound like the Council. Don't you know how to show love anymore? Or is that too dangerous for you, making yourself vulnerable? Why can't you just once let go?"

"Shut up!" he cried in pain. "How can you understand how I feel, how hard it is to fill Father's shoes like Stephen did."

"Well, I have to take Mother's place," she retorted. "To try and understand what a little boy needs."

She pushed him aside and picked me up. "There now," she crooned. "It'll be all right. I'll take care of you. I've been so wrapped up in my own feelings, I forgot you, Jael. I'm so sorry. All this is really too much for you to understand."

Her voice was soft and soothing as she talked into the night. I knew she was saying those things more for herself, but just hearing the sound of her voice helped me. She was still sitting on the bed rocking me when the sky began to redden in the west.

After that, Darien went back to his old ways of keeping to himself. He was very quiet and never smiled. When school was over and our meal was finished, he retreated to his room and played his manitar. Sometimes I'd sit and listen the way I used to, but he took no notice of me, seeming to go into a trance when he played.

I was getting taller now, so I could help Martina with cleaning after the evening meal and when she was tidying the house. Stephen used to help her with these, and she seemed glad of my assistance. We didn't talk much, though. It was just too hard to think of what to say. Gradually, things became calmer for my sister and me. I could sleep through the night again without having nightmares. But Darien's quiet was about to explode.

It happened one night just after we'd eaten. Darien began to play so loudly in his room that we could hear the music clearly. Then suddenly there came a terrible crash and the sound of breaking wood and twanging strings. A mangled manitar crashed down the spiral staircase. Behind it came Darien, stomping his feet.

"It's no good!" he shouted.

"What's no good?" I asked.

"Anything! Everything!" His voice was an anguished cry.

"It's no good retreating into yourself, you mean." The tone in Martina's voice surprised me, so cold and hard. I'd never heard her sound like this.

"You never have understood!" he cried.

"I understand you're still trying to hide from yourself, big brother!"

"Don't condemn me so quickly," he sneered. "You're hiding, too, in your own way. Behind Jael perhaps?" He almost spit these words out. "Well, I'm not hiding anymore, if that's any satisfaction to you. I'm going to do *something!*"

He was almost out the door by this time, and we ran after him.

"Don't leave us, Darien!" I cried.

"What *are* you going to do?" asked Martina.

"I don't know yet," he called over his shoulder. "Maybe I'll join the Star Corps."

"You know they only take firstborn," she yelled after him.

He just kept on heading down the street, acting as though he hadn't heard her.

For the next two days, Martina stayed home with me and didn't go to school. She said she didn't want me to be alone, but I doubted this was really the reason. I had Anha and Raina to go to, but perhaps Martina needed me. She even read to me from the books, though by this time I could read most of them for myself.

The second night Darien returned, wearing the pale gray uniform of the Inland Raiders.

"Not bad, huh?" he said, flaunting the uniform for us. "Maybe the Star Corps wouldn't take me, but I found a place for myself. The Inland Raiders are the real backbone of the armies."

"You look grand," I said. "Almost like S-" I found that Stephen's name caught in my throat.

"Only almost?" said Darien, with a hint of disappointment in his voice.

"No! You look fine," I said quickly. "Please tell me about Inland Raiders. What do they do?"

"Let's sit down first."

Martina brought some hot spiced moffee, as we all settled down on the cushions. She didn't speak at all until after Darien finished his long, glowing descriptions. From what I could gather, the Inland Raiders were a special team who were sent on secret missions into enemy territory. Though they didn't pilot their own ships—the Star Corps had to do that—they still had an important role.

"These are Galactic Wars," he said, "Because they move back and forth across the Galaxy, wherever Rebels are. You never know what will happen next because pockets of Rebels can turn up anywhere. That's why the Inland Raiders are so special. We have more contact with the enemy than any other unit."

"But who are the real Rebels?" Martina finally spoke. "Are they loyal to old Earth and the King who reigns there, like Father used to tell us? How can you tell who the real enemy is?"

"Martina, it's a complicated Galaxy," he replied. "This isn't just a story in one of your old books, with good guys and bad guys. Do you really think it's as simple as Father told us when we were children? No one I know has ever seen this King. Is he even real?"

"Oh, I don't know anymore, either!" she cried. "I get more and more confused every time I think about it. But just remember, everywhere you go with your Raiders, you'll be depending on a Star Corps voyager to get you there."

"So what?" I could tell Darien didn't like being reminded of this. As he spoke again, his eyes seemed to be pleading with me, "Jael will be proud of me, won't you?"

I nodded and reached for his hand. He didn't draw back from my touch as he often did. Then something began to trouble me. "Will you be gone for a long time?" I asked.

"Yes, I'm afraid so. In fact, for my training mission, I may be gone for two or three passes around Regelian."

"Two or three! That's so long. I'll be old before you come back."

"If I even come back that soon, Jael. There may be another mission right after the training."

"I knew it!" Martina cried suddenly. "You just couldn't face staying and trying to help us, or facing the Council again. So you're going far away where you can be with aliens and rebels and not have to worry about Jael and me."

There were tears in her eyes now, and Darien's voice softened when he saw this. "Please try to understand. I can only do the best I can. I'm not Father or Stephen. And I'm the only one left to earn us some financial support."

"But there has to be some other way," she said, as her tears began to spill over. "Whatever happened to standing together as a family? You're letting the Council keep on separating us one by one."

"It's too late, Martina. I've made my decision. My ship leaves tomorrow morning, if you care to see me off." He started up the staircase.

"Are you staying tonight?" she asked.

"No. I have to gather some belongings. Then I'll be sleeping at the crew quarters."

"How can you do this to us?" she cried suddenly. She was on her feet and shaking her fist at him. Before he could answer, the door slammed and she was gone from the house.

I was sitting in the same spot where they'd left me when he came back down. Setting down his bundle, he knelt in front of me and lifted my chin in his hands.

"I hope you'll understand all of this someday, Jael."

I nodded and felt the tears beginning to come again. Then I threw my arms around his neck and clung to him, wanting to feel the comfort of his embrace just once more. I squeezed him so tightly he had to pry me loose.

"Hey now," he whispered, "Everything will be okay. I'll be taking care of you, sending the credits to help you guys pay your debts here. Maybe I can even send you a present sometime."

Still, I clung to him. "It's a strange way to take care of people, to go far away like Father did."

"Shh, little brother. Tears won't help."

But I couldn't stop crying.

"Come on, and I'll put you to bed. Martina will be home soon to feed you."

Once I was in bed and looking up at him, he looked very tall and strong, but already far away, especially in his eyes. "Martina just doesn't understand, Jael. She thinks I'm trying to discipline my mind this way. But I'm not giving in to the Council or the Underground. I'm just trying to find my own way, a balance, like Father and Stephen said."

Then he kissed me on the forehead and said, "Life is full of farewells, Jael. I don't know if they ever end."

I closed my eyes then. When I opened them, he was gone.

I must have lain there a very long time, the tears still flowing. The room grew darker as the first moon set. Still Martina hadn't come, and now I was hungry. Just as I finally decided to find some food myself, I heard the door open.

A very strange sound wafted up to me. Mystified, I crept to the top of the stairs. Martina was laughing in an odd way and leaning heavily on someone, as though she couldn't stand on her own. When the light fell on his hair, I knew it was Jason.

"Nobody's home anymore, Jason-sweetie," she giggled in a silly way. "You can do with me as you please, just like in the Underground. I'm all yours."

He held her close and kissed her for a very long time. Then they sank to the floor, and I saw he was taking her tunic off. I closed my eyes at the sight of her nakedness, but I could still hear them. When I finally opened my eyes, I could see him lying beside her, his eyes closed.

In a daze, I crept back to bed, feeling very strange. This was an adult thing I'd seen, I knew, and I wasn't sure what to think. I just wished there was some way to get my sister back for myself, but it looked like she belonged to Jason now.

***

When I crept down the staircase in the early light of morning, Jason was gone, and she lay on the floor with her tunic over her like a blanket. I had to shake her a long time before she would wake.

"Go away!" she muttered.

"Martina, please. I'm hungry!"

"My head hurts too much," she moaned. "I drank too much ale last night."

"Please get up!" I cried again. "We have to see Darien off at the spaceport."

"Darien? Oh yeah—I don't care. You go."

"Martina, please! I can't get there by myself."

"Oh okay. Make moffee and I'll get up."

"You promise?"

"Promise," she muttered, rolling onto her other side and burying her head in the cushion.

I'd never made moffee before, but I'd watched, so I did the best I could. It must have been good enough, for Martina finally sat up and gazed at me with bleary eyes when she smelled it.

"Good boy, Jael. Good brother—only one I've got left."

I didn't like the sound of these mutterings, but I tried to shrug them off and get her up from the floor. It took a lot of pushing and prodding to keep her going. I was afraid we'd miss the lift-off, so I kept pestering her until we finally got down the street to catch the Tube to the spaceport. And we got there just barely in time.

"Stay back!" a guard shouted at us, as we approached the visitor's gate. "This area is restricted to passengers and families."

"Yes, my brother is out there!" I cried.

"They're already boarding," he said. "All you can do now is wave, and hope he sees you."

So I started waving for all I was worth, and shouting Darien's name.

"He can't hear you," said Martina. "Save your voice."

But I kept on yelling. Then a dark head turned toward us and began to wave back, and I knew it was Darien. Soon he disappeared into the hold of the ship.

"He saw us," I said to my sister.

"Yes, he did see us after all."

Suddenly she became more animated than I'd seen in a long time. She grabbed my hand and pulled me toward the outside gate. "Come on!" she cried.

"Where are you going? I want to see the lift-off."

"But I know a place where we can see the very last of the ship as it leaves the planet."

"Neptune Spire?"

"Yes."

"But there's no time. And I want to stay here close to Darien."

"We can't do both, Jael," she said in exasperation.

The guard apparently was listening to this because he walked up to us. I was afraid he was going to tell us to leave, but instead he said, "I have an idea for you kids. How about a compromise? I know how it feels to have family going so far away. I'll take you up to the observation tower over there." He pointed to a very tall tower just inside the restricted area. It wasn't as high as Neptune Spire, but it was very tall.

I looked at Martina, questioning, and she nodded. The guard left for a moment and when he came back, he let us inside the gate. Soon we were whooshing to the top of the tower in a lift.

There were some men up there, looking at rows of lights on panels, but there were also a few family members like us, standing near the thick plastiglas windows. We were barely in time, for steam was billowing in great clouds from the base of the rocket. Then a yellow-white flame appeared and grew huge very suddenly.

Ever so slowly the ship began to rise, and then it was moving faster than we could have imagined. In two breaths, it was high above us. Martina tugged at my arm and pointed at one of the panels nearby, where a screen showed a picture of the ship as it rose higher and higher. I wanted to see the real thing, though, the ship where my brother was riding. By this time, it was just a tiny speck of color against the blue of the Terres sky. Then it was only a bright spot of light.

I watched until my eyes ached, and tried not to blink. I'm sure I didn't, but it was as though I did, for suddenly the light winked and was gone. It faded like a song fades away—you can't pinpoint the instant the last note ends and becomes only memory.

That was all we had left of our family—memory. I slipped my hand into my sister's and tried to smile up at her. Her smile was as weak as mine, and her eyes were shining like mine were, with tears. Perhaps it was true, as Darien said, that farewells never end. But right then I tried not to think of this. I wasn't sure we could take any more.

CHAPTER 10

THE OLD WAYS

After Darien left, Martina sent me to school. This hadn't been the plan before, but she didn't seem to care anymore. She said we couldn't keep paying Anha to watch me. And I could tell she didn't want to be stuck at home with me all the time. The hardest part for me was not getting to see Raina anymore.

The silence in the house became harder and harder to bear. Martina still prepared meals and I helped clean, but we had even less to say than before. Her eyes usually had a strange faraway look in them, and when she did talk it was about her dreams of finding a new place. I didn't understand how we could afford to live anywhere but in Terres-City. There were no other cities on the planet, and we weren't allowed to ride the space ships without Stephen.

When she was home and the work was done, she'd usually sit at the west window gazing out. And she often stared at Stephen's urn far into the night.

At school, they were surprised I could read and write in the old way, actually using paper. Almost everyone, tutors and students alike, laughed at me. It was the first time I fully realized how different my family was. Now I began to understand the way Martina, Darien, and Stephen were treated when they'd been at school. And some of the conversations I'd heard when I was young began to make sense to me. I kept wondering why my parents thought it so important to collect those old books, and why they refused to have a Terminal in our house.

So I asked Martina, because she was the only person I had left.

"Well, Jael," she said, "Father always said old ways aren't necessarily bad, like the Council teaches. Some new ways are good, too, but that's no reason to throw out the old. It's better to have both. Balance was a word Father used a lot," she added. "You know, it really is too bad you have no memories of Father."

Then I decided I'd try to find my own balance, too. I told my tutor I wanted to learn to use the Terminal, and he was pleased with how quickly I progressed.

"You're very bright, Jael," he said. "Soon you'll catch up with others your age. You may even pass them."

One time the tutor said something which really surprised me. We were alone at the Terminal, playing a game called Space Docking, which involved doing all the proper calculations and maneuvers to effect a smooth docking of a space shuttle with an orbiting station. There were many factors and motions to consider, and he praised me for how well I did.

"You have a real talent for working with space craft, Jael," he said. "Maybe you'll be able to work in space someday."

"But the Star Corps won't take me," I said.

"No, but there are other solar systems and other ways of doing things," he whispered.

My eyes grew wide as he continued, "It's true. The Council and System officials of Terres don't have the exclusive and only right way of doing things. Your family must have realized this, since they taught you to read ancient books and texts. That may pay off for you someday. In other worlds, you'd be much better prepared to adjust than anyone from Terres. You'll be able to select and sort information for yourself, instead of depending on a Terminal to do it for you. You'll be able to put your own thoughts into written words so you can communicate them to others."

"But how can I ever find places like that?" I asked

"Well, there are the Redlarks,"

Just then a tall girl entered the room and seated herself at another station of the Terminal. My tutor looked frightened for an instant. Then he said in a normal voice, "Well, let's try that docking one more time. You almost have it."

He never said anything more about books or Redlarks. After this conversation, I had so many more unanswered questions I longed to ask, but we never had a chance to talk like that again. Once I had an idea to invite him to come to our house, so I could show him our books.

"I'd love to, Jael," he said softly. "But it's not permitted. I'm sorry."

I was sorry, too. I could sense he was afraid, and never brought the subject up again. So, I turned to the only person I knew who might answer some of my questions, Martina.

She'd finally stopped staring at the urn all the time and started reading books again. A semblance of peace came back to the house.

One evening, just as the first moon was rising, she was reading as usual. There was a hint of a smile on her lips, and she seemed to be in a good mood so I decided now would be my best chance.

"Martina?"

"Hmm?"

"I know Jason told you about Redlarks. What are they?"

She looked up suddenly, slammed the book closed, and her green eyes bored into me. "Why do you want to know?" There was a sharp edge in her voice.

"Well, my tutor at school was talking about books one day. I asked, how could there be a place with no Terminals here on Terres, and he said, there were the Redlarks. But he couldn't, or wouldn't, tell me anymore."

At this her face became calmer and she looked at me

intently for a long time. "I guess you're old enough to know now," she said at last. "But you must never tell anyone these things. I don't think Father ever meant for Mother to tell us." Then out of the blue, she said the strangest thing:

"Our father had a twin brother who was born just before him."

"What? He couldn't have. Stephen told me Father was in the Star Corps, and they only take firstborn."

"That's true."

"But how can it be then? The Council wouldn't make a mistake. And what's this got to do with Redlarks?"

"If you'll stop asking so many questions, I'll tell you."

"Okay." I bit my lip, not wanting to make her angry.

But her eyes weren't angry. They were beginning to get that strange look they had when Raina asked Jason about Redlarks on Neptune Spire.

"The Council didn't make a mistake," she said. "At least, they didn't think so. They made our father firstborn of his family because his brother ran away to the Redlarks. Anyone who goes to the Redlarks is declared nonexistent, as though they'd never been born. No one is ever to speak his or her name again. So Father became firstborn by Council decree."

"But what's so terrible about the Redlarks?"

"I don't know. People won't talk about them. But I don't think Father thought they were all bad. Sometimes I think he wondered if he should have gone with his brother."

"Maybe he didn't die!" I cried suddenly. "Maybe he went to the Redlarks, and the Council only said he died."

"No, Jael. He really did die in the Galactic Wars. It wasn't like Father to run away like his brother Dominic did. He didn't agree with the Council and the System, but he decided to stay and live a life he hoped would help others to see the truth—to try to change things from the inside. So, he went where the Star Corps sent him—and he was killed."

"Stephen was like Father, wasn't he?"

"Yes, he was. Maybe because he was named after him. At least through him you got a glimpse of what Father was like. They both tried to do what seemed right to them, working slowly from the inside instead of leaving to find a life somewhere else. But I'm not sure I can be like them."

"But Martina, I still don't understand what Redlarks are."

"Well, they're people from Terres-City who don't like being ruled by the Council. They eat food they grow themselves, have their own chiefs and leaders, and their own ways. Some say they're barbarians who live in the Wilds, but I wonder. All their ways may not be right, but sometimes I think I'd like to find out for myself."

She was looking at Stephen's urn again. "I wonder if the Redlarks would have made you cremate him," I whispered.

"Maybe not. But it's too late now."

"I wonder if they have books, too."

"I don't know," she shrugged. "Rarely, people try to come back, I've heard. Jason says he knows someone named Jon, who's come back to the city from the Redlarks. But he won't tell me any more. He says I am getting too many rebellious ideas."

My head was whirling around all these thoughts. For some reason, I desperately wanted to meet this Jon. But I wasn't sure how it could ever happen. I decided to ask Martina more questions while she was in a good mood.

"Martina, is that why we have books—because of Father's brother?"

"I think so. It was Father's way of not forgetting him. And I think Father wanted to help us remember something of the old ways, and where our ancestors really came from—Earth. He taught us to read and made us promise to teach you."

"I'm really glad you did teach me, Martina."

"Even though the others have laughed at you in school?"

I merely nodded.

"Well, I'm glad I could help you, then."

"Yes, I want to know even more about these old ways. I wish I could meet this Jon. Do you think *we* might go to the Redlarks?"

"I don't know if it's a good idea or not," she whispered.

We sat for a long time in silence. I snuggled close to her, happy we still were together.

"You know Jael," she finally said, "I don't know if I should tell you this, but you've always reminded me of Stephen and Father. Not just your looks, though. Somehow you have a special aura like they did. I can't explain it. It's sort of a vibration or something."

Her words tapered off into silence again.

I didn't know what to say.

***

That was a very special evening. It rarely happened we could talk so much about the things bounding around in my mind. But after that talk, she seemed to draw farther away again, as though her own thoughts were troubling her. I wanted to help her, but didn't know what to say. She seemed to want to read every book in the house, and since there was little else to do after school, I joined her with a book of my own, sitting beside the window. We seldom spoke, though.

When she wasn't reading, she was with Jason. Some days she was still sitting in the window when I went to school. I wasn't sure she was even going to school anymore. But she was older than me, so maybe she was finished.

Nearly every night, she'd put on a special tunic Jason

had given her, and fix her dark hair gathered up in curls on the top of her head, "the way Jason likes it," she always said.

Once when I was watching her preparations, I asked, "Where do you go with Jason?"

Her eyes began to dance strangely in her reflection in the mirror. "Oh, we go Underground where no one can find us—and we fly!"

"Are you just teasing, Martina? How can you fly under the ground?"

"Oh silly! It *just feels* like flying. Wait until you're older, then you'll understand."

Every night now, she and Jason would be gone for hours. Often, they didn't come back until the early morning sun was rising, and she had a silly laugh and unsteadiness in her walk.

Some nights when Jason came, they went up to her room, closing the door instead of going out. He didn't leave until morning. I tried to pretend I was asleep and couldn't hear them, but their voices came through the walls, and as the night grew late, I'd hear the deep sighs and other strange sounds they made. I felt very alone, like I'd lost my sister to someone else. I tried to sleep, but I never could until silence settled over them. I felt a deep heaviness in my chest and wished something would change. I couldn't stand the thought of going on living like this in loneliness.

One night Jason didn't come, and she sat alone in the window, reading the ancient black book with only the title

"The Book" written across its cover. Her brow seemed to furrow in worry as she read. She sighed deeply, and when I looked up, I could see tears shining in her eyes.

"What's the matter, 'Tina?" I asked.

This was the name Stephen always used for her. I hoped she'd open up to me more if I used it.

But she just brushed angrily at her tears and shrugged, "Nothing."

"Please, don't shut me out." I felt my voice catch in my throat. "I'm still your brother, even if I'm the smallest. Please talk to me."

She attempted a weak smile. "I'm glad you're here, Jael," she said softly.

"But what's wrong? Why are you crying?"

She sighed again. "Oh, I'm just confused, I guess. I keep trying to remember what Stephen told me about the Underground and love. But the feelings I have with Jason are so strong I can't seem to sort them out. I just get swept away with him. I'm one person before he comes, but when we get to the Underground I become someone I don't even recognize—someone who does things I know aren't right. I get caught up in the passions, and think I feel good. But afterwards in the light of day, I feel ashamed and don't even know why. I tell myself, 'I won't do that again,' but when the time comes I do it anyway and can't stop myself."

"I wish there was something I could do to help you," I whispered.

"So do I, Jael. But this is way beyond you."

"Why are things getting so complicated now that Darien and Stephen are gone?" I sighed. "Why are we getting confused about things that used to make sense?"

"I don't know, Jael. I think it's the way the Council tries to control people. And sometimes I think it would be easier to just let go and be told what to think and believe, instead of always trying to figure it out for ourselves. I wish we didn't live on this planet!" she cried suddenly.

"But we don't have any choice in that."

"I wonder..." she began softly. But then she lapsed into silence and wouldn't say any more.

The next time Jason came, they crept into her room as usual. At first, I could hear their voices talking softly. I was lying in my bed, and actually dozed off, when there came a sudden loud crash like something being thrown.

Then Jason's voice rang out, "You and your old ways! You seem to think that all the new is bad and only the old is good."

"That's not true! Didn't I go to the Underground with you?"

"But now you just want to stay here."

"Because we can be more alone here, and-"

"All you talk about is how old ways are better," he interrupted. "Like how it would been better to bury your brother. I'm sick of all this moping. Stephen's dead—just forget him. Let his body rest in the dust, so his mind can be free."

"I'll never let go of my family!" she cried. "And don't you talk about my brother anymore."

"And then you break all the rules and want to talk about the Redlarks," his voice went on, even louder now. "So go ahead—why don't you just join them—live like a barbarian instead of in the comforts of the City. See if I care!"

"What good are the comforts of the City if there's no meaning in my life? I can't go on like this! Trying to get up every day, when it feels like there's nothing worth living for. I'm not like you—I can't just sit back and let the Council tell me where to go, what to do, what to think, and how to live."

I'd never heard my sister's voice sound so strong with anger before.

"And I guess our relationship is nothing, either!" Jason shouted then. "Don't I mean anything in your life?"

"What meaning?" she shouted back. "You think it's so special, letting myself get carried away in lust? You think you can be very disciplined in the light of day, and as wanton as you like at night. I can't go on living two lives like that."

"Now I see it!" he cried. "You never have understood what the Council has accomplished. I guess you're too polluted with your family's old ways. I tried to help you, to keep you away from those who would punish you, but now I can see it's hopeless. Don't blame me for what happens next. I've had enough. Don't come crying to me anymore. I won't be around."

I crept to my door just in time to see Martina's door fly open. Jason was pulling on his shirt as he stomped down the stairs. My sister's eyes were very red, and so was her face. But she just glared at me and slammed her door shut.

Her door was still closed the next morning when I got up. Not a sound came from her room as I got some moffee prepared, and gathered my things for school. I left a cup of the hot liquid on the table for her and went to catch the Tube.

When I came home, I had a strange feeling something was wrong as soon as I opened the outer door. Everything looked the same, including the moffee on the table. It hadn't been touched. My throat began to tighten.

"Martina?" I called.

Silence answered me.

My heart was beginning to pound. Then I saw Stephen's urn, lying on its side—empty. Beginning to shake, I moved to the table by the window. A fine dusting of ash covered the top, except for one square where an old box had set. My finger was trembling as I touched the ash, all I had left of my eldest brother.

Then tears began to pour from my eyes, and I could hear myself sobbing as I sank to the floor. "Oh, Stephen!" I cried. "What do I do now? I'm the only one left."

CHAPTER 11

LIONS AND FEIER-CATS

I was still lying on the floor when the sound of the door opening woke me. The room was dark around me, and then a light beamed across the floor.

"Jael!" said Jason's voice. "What's wrong?"

He came over and lifted me gently. "Are you hurt? Where's Martina?"

I just shook my head mutely as he set me on a cushion.

"I came to tell her I was sorry for last night. I guess you heard."

I nodded again.

"I didn't mean to get so angry, Jael. I just don't understand her sometimes."

"It's too late," I blurted out suddenly. "She's gone to the Redlarks."

"Nonsense. She wouldn't really do that."

"But she's taken Stephen's ashes with her in a box. And where else would she go?"

His mouth was hanging open as he followed my gaze to the overturned urn. "You must be mistaken," he said. "She'll come back soon, don't worry. She's gone off to be alone for awhile." He sounded like he was trying to convince himself as much as me.

I tried to nod, but I knew she wouldn't be back. Then I began to wonder how much truth there was in his angry words of the night before, especially the threat, 'Don't come to me…' Did he really regret those words now, or had he only come back to check on the response to them?

Then some words Stephen once said began to echo in my mind, 'Jael is the one they want.'

Suddenly I realized Jason was shaking me. "Jael, can you hear me?"

I managed to look up at him, but my fear of him was growing.

"You can't stay here alone," he said. "Why don't you come home with me?"

"No. I mean—I should stay here in case Martina comes back."

For an instant, his eyes seemed to flash with anger. Then he shrugged and looked away. "Have it your way, then. But don't say I didn't warn you."

There it was again, words that were almost a threat, hovering at the edge of my understanding like a mist. Or was I only imagining it?

"I'll be all right," I said, trying to keep my voice calm and even. "I know how to fix my own meals."

He shrugged again and started for the door. As he opened it, he turned as if he were going to say something else, but then just waved his hand in dismissal. The door hissed closed behind him.

***

For a few days, I tried to keep myself in some kind of normal pattern, but it was very difficult. At school, I'd just stare at the walls when I was supposed to be working at the Terminal. I began to fall behind in my lessons.

At home, I fixed a small meal, but seldom ate it all. I just stared at the food, or watched as my tears fell in a small puddle on the plate. The house was so lonely and silent it left me totally empty inside.

One day, as I came from the Tube station, I saw black smoke drifting toward me. Then I realized with a shock that it was coming out the gaping front door of my house. Had I left something burning in the galley? Before I even thought what to do, my feet were running toward that open door.

Inside, the house was full of choking smoke, but I ran in anyway, waving my arms. By opening the windows, I got the air to clear some. Then I saw the awful mess. Everything in the place was turned upside-down or inside-out. Plants lay mutilated and exposed in the garden room, ripped from their pots. All the food in the galley was thrown on the floor and stomped on.

But the worst part was in the front room where all the books were pulled from their shelves, piled up, and burned. They were still smoldering, but not one was left readable. All were blackened. Someone was very careful in making sure every page burned. It was just as bad in the upstairs rooms—everything turned into confusion—probably as they'd searched for every piece of paper and print in the house. Whoever *they* were, and however they'd found out about us. Jason's threatening words came back to me again, and I began to wonder if he'd betrayed us.

I don't even remember how I got there, but I found myself lying on my bed, staring at the ceiling. My mind seemed to be just one aching cry, 'Why?'

As I lay wondering what to do now, my eyes fell on the floor along the back edge of my bed. There, plastered tightly against the wall, was a small piece of paper they'd missed. I recognized it at once as a little pamphlet of passages from The Book. Vaguely, I remembered reading it in bed one night. It must have slipped down there and been lost for a long time.

I opened it, and the page turned to the story of Daniel and the Den of Lions. I reached into my pocket and pulled out the frayed slip of paper Stephen had given me before our shuttle trip, tucking it into a little pocket in the back of the pamphlet. Then, without thinking what I was doing, or why, I closed the pamphlet and stuffed it inside my undershirt, next to my skin where no one could see it.

In the same instant, I sensed someone standing in the doorway, glaring at me. Looking up, I was shocked to see Jason.

"Did you know about this?" I cried.

He was shaking his head, speaking deeply and evenly, "Most unfortunate, isn't it? Must have been vandals. Now do you see why you can't stay here alone? After all, you're still just a child."

I tried to listen to his words, but something in his voice made me wonder if he believed them himself. And my own thoughts kept echoing in my mind, 'The Council must be behind this. They've done just what my brothers said—drawn us apart one by one. Jason could even be part of the plan.'

"Jael, you have only two choices, come with me or be put in the rehabilitation center. I'm really trying to help you. Will you come with me or not?"

My mind was racing. 'Mother was taken to a rehabilitation center, but the odds of finding her are almost none. But I'm not sure if I'll be safe with Jason, either. He's scaring me more each time I see him. Still, perhaps in his own way he really is trying to help. And if I go with him, I can see Raina again.' That was the only hopeful note in all this mess.

So, feeling totally helpless and with Raina as my only hope, I let Jason lead me out of the devastated house. Even as I left, I knew somehow I'd never see it again.

***

So that's how I came to live with Raina and Jason. I wanted to say they were a family like mine, but right away I could tell they weren't. There was little playing games or talking together and, of course, no books to read. They ate together sometimes, but even that was rare. Each person—Raina, Jason, or their parents—would select their own tray-meal and pop it into the micro to warm it. Each ate by themselves when they felt like it. No one paid much attention to anyone else.

They had a Terminal in every room, and you could do schoolwork or listen to Council programs with pictures. In the evening, each person in the house would go to their own room and listen to their Terminal. It was as though they were in their own cubicle or cell. I began to feel more alone here than in my own empty house.

Sometimes late in the night, when I was sure no one could see, I'd slip out my little pamphlet and read some of its words, "For we know that all things work together for good to them that love God, who are called according to His purpose."

Those words seemed to give me a little hope. I couldn't

see how any of these things happening to me could turn out for good, but still I hoped those words were true.

Another night I found these words, "Beloved, now we are the sons of God, and it doesn't yet appear what we shall be; but we know that when He shall appear, we shall be like Him; for we shall see Him as He is."

I wondered who it was that was supposed to appear. What was he like? What did it mean, we would be like him? These words made me feel strange deep inside, like something was going to happen to me someday—something wonderful.

For a long time after I went to Raina's, I didn't go to school. In fact, I didn't feel like doing anything. I probably would have read a book if there had been any in the house. Instead I just sat and stared out the window, watching Regelian rise and cross the sky west to east until it faded into night.

When Raina came home from school, she'd sit beside me often and hold my hand. I knew she was there and was glad, but I seldom spoke to her. I guess I was afraid of saying the wrong thing, wondering if I could trust anyone. My mind seemed numb, and I felt I had to protect myself from further hurt by drawing into a shell.

Then one day, she brought a small bundle to me, laying it on my lap as she sat down beside me.

"Open it," she said softly.

My hands moved slowly, and I kept glancing at her questioningly. Then the wrapping fell away. Inside, was a little animal making tiny mewing sounds. It nuzzled my hand, and I felt its rough tongue give me a little lick.

"It's a feier-cat," Raina said. "This one is still a baby. It'll grow bigger, to about two hands long. They live in the Wilds of Terres—they told me at the store. But this one is tame. He'll be your friend."

I tried to smile at her and finally managed to find some words, "Is he really mine, then?"

"Yes, a gift from me."

Tears came to my eyes, unbidden. She reached up her hand and brushed one off my cheek.

"Go ahead and cry if it helps, Jael."

"Thanks, Raina."

Having the little feier-cat to care for forced me to come out of my shell. Besides, he provided some company. He looked much like ancient pictures I'd seen of cats, his fur soft and a mottled mix of brown, white, and tan. There was one difference, though—he had wings. They were tiny now and folded back over his shoulders, folds of velvety skin stretched over delicate bones. I wondered if he could really fly with them; they hardly looked like they would support his weight.

When he was hungry, he'd let out plaintive cries, but when he was happy, he'd sit on my lap and make a humming sound. It was almost like music. It seemed he even understood my words when I spoke to him. And so, another thing the feier-cat did was to get me talking again.

I looked up feier-cats on the Terminal and found out the first settlers on Terres had named them for an ancient word meaning 'joyful.' This was because of a peculiar upturn of their lips which made them look like they were always smiling. I decided there was no better name for my new pet than Feier, because he'd brought a little joy back into my life.

Soon I even went back to school and worked to catch up in my studies. Some calm returned to my life, but I wasn't content. I knew deep inside where Martina had gone, even though Jason and Raina refused to believe me. Maybe they were still hoping she'd turn up and not have to be declared non-existent by the Council. For myself, I knew the only answer was to find a way to follow her into the Wilds.

One day I dared to tell Raina of my plan.

"You can't go into the Wilds all by yourself," she hissed. "You could get lost, or starve, or be eaten by beasts."

"I could take Feier with me. He's a creature of the Wilds."

"But he was born in a cage. He's never seen the Wilds, any more than you have."

"Then I'll wait until he gets older," I shrugged.

When Raina saw she couldn't change my mind, she decided to find a way to help. One day, when no one else was around, she said, "You at least need to learn more about the Wilds and the Redlarks. Like where to go to find them, for one thing."

"But how can I do that? No one will talk about them. Not even Jason."

"Well, Jason has a friend named Jon, who he says came back from the Redlarks."

"Yeah, Martina told me that, too. But how do I get *his* help?"

"I'm not sure, but next time he comes to see Jason, we'll talk to him."

So, I waited impatiently for the mysterious Jon to appear. It seemed impossible anyone could go to the Redlarks and come back—it was like someone coming back from the dead. Raina confirmed this, too. "Jon can never go back to his real home or family," she said. "He had to become another person in disguise. It must be terribly lonely."

I nodded, for I knew how lonely felt.

One day as we were coming in after school, Raina suddenly jerked my arm sharply.

"Ouch!"

"Sh! He's here."

"Jon? Where?"

"I hear his voice. He's talking in Jason's room."

I could hear the faint rumble of their voices but could distinguish no words. Then the two of them came out of the room. Jon was taller than Jason, with blond, wavy hair. Two things were striking about him—he was very thin and wiry, and his eyes were a strange color, a deep brown that looked almost violet. And now those eyes seemed to be looking right through me.

"Jon," Raina was saying, "This is my friend, Jael. He wanted to meet you."

"Hello," he said, but his manner seemed preoccupied, and he walked right on by with Jason.

Before I could open my mouth to speak, they'd gone out the door. I felt crushed with disappointment. Then Raina's hand was in mine.

"Hey, don't worry. We'll talk to him next time. At least now he knows you."

I nodded and tried to swallow the lump in my throat.

After this, Raina and I started going to Neptune Spire after school almost every day. That way I could look out at the Wilds. I'd stand for what seemed hours, just staring at the green hills below the Peaks, as though by looking long enough I might see something that would lead me to Martina. But all I ever saw was the changing of the light and colors as Regelian sank into the east. And some days when it was especially clear I could see the jagged, towering peaks, so far away that they looked like paper cutouts hung around the rim of the world.

When Feier was old enough, I started taking him with me. I made a pack that I could carry over my shoulders, so he rode on my back in the bag, peeking out over the top. When no one else was near us at the top of the spire, I would talk to him softly, telling of the Wilds and my vow to find my sister. I had an uncanny feeling he understood every word.

We sometimes saw Jon at the spire, right before sunset. When I noticed this, I made it a point to be there at the same time. He always seemed to look toward the east, where the peaks were highest and most rugged. I wondered if there was something special about that direction, something about Redlarks.

For a long time, Jon acted as though he didn't recognize me. Then finally he began to nod a silent hello. Once he even said, "Hello. Are you Jason's friend?"

"Yes, I'm Jael, his sister's friend."

That was the extent of our conversation for a long time. Finally, one day when Raina was with me, I gathered my courage. "I'm going to just come right out and ask him, Raina."

"Don't be silly. He won't talk if you start it," she hissed. "Not about forbidden places here in public."

"I can't stand it any longer," I whispered back. "If I spend my whole life waiting, I'll never find my sister."

Jon was leaning against a railing not far away, so I

moved toward him as casually as I could. I was close beside him and just about to speak when his voice came to me, "Hello, Jael."

I was so surprised my breath left me. There I stood with my mouth open trying to reply, but no words came. His next words almost floored me.

"Your sister has gone to the Redlarks, hasn't she? And you want to find her?"

My knees began to quiver, but I managed to nod. It seemed he could hear my thoughts.

"You'd better try to forget her. She'll be declared non-existent. She can't come back. I shouldn't have come back myself."

I could feel pain welling up inside my chest. "But she's the only family I have left. I need her."

"She's gone forever," he hissed, turning abruptly on his heel and walking away. As his lean form disappeared into the core of the tower, I could feel the tears trickling down my cheeks. Raina reached for my hand.

"I tried to warn you," she said.

"But I didn't even say anything. It was like he could read my mind."

"Well," she shrugged, "I've always thought he was very strange."

That night was a bad one for me. As I lay in bed, I kept seeing Stephen's face as clearly as if he were right there with me. It was impossible to believe I'd never see him again. Pictures flashed in my mind—Stephen laughing and riding me on his shoulders, showing me pictures of the Star Corps, and then that last dreadful look at him laid out on the cold stone.

Waking pictures mingled with dreams as I tossed and turned, finally to wake shivering in a cold sweat. Then the pictures would change to Darien or Martina, and I'd ache with longing to see one of them again. Feier must have sensed something was wrong, for he crept up from his spot at the foot of the bed and nestled close beside me. I stroked his fur and rubbed under his chin the way he liked.

"Oh, Feier," I murmured, "If only you could talk to me."

'I can.' Those words were in my mind as clearly as if someone said them audibly.

"Is that you, Feier?" I asked in a mere whisper.

'Yes.'

"How can that be? Are you really talking to me?"

'I am. Jon has taught me.'

"Jon? How?"

'Whenever he's near me, he talks to me in the mind just like this.'

I was dumbfounded and stared at the little feier-cat, wondering if this was all part of one of my dreams.

'You aren't dreaming,' came the immediate reply from Feier. 'I'm really here in your mind.'

"Can you *read* my mind then?" I asked.

'Only what you express in words, spoken or unspoken.'

"So that's how Jon knows about Martina!"

'Yes, through me, he knows all you've told me.'

I sat still, almost unbelieving. Feier nudged my hand with his head, as he did when he wanted petting. I rubbed absently behind his ears.

'You should sleep now,' he said. 'I'll be right here.'

I curled up with Feier cuddled in the space between my knees and chin, and finally did sleep for the rest of the night.

***

In the morning, clean light from Regelian was washing the walls in white. I blinked and almost felt glad for the new day. Then I remembered the strange experience of the night before and wondered if it was just a dream. Feier was sitting up at the foot of the bed, gazing at me with silvery eyes and seeming to smile.

"Good morning, Feier," I said softly.

'Good morning, Jael.'

Just like last night! It was true then. I bounded out of bed, smiling and humming a tune–something I hadn't done for a long time. Somehow, this new communication with Feier gave me hope. Perhaps I could get through to Jon now, with Feier's help.

But the next few times I went to Neptune Spire, Jon wasn't there. First, I feared he'd left the city again, or perhaps decided to avoid me after my boldness in approaching him. I began to feel very restless. The only thing that kept me from taking off for the Wilds immediately was Feier.

'Jon kept saying something about a sign at sunset,' he said. 'It was almost as if he could see the future.'

"Has it happened yet?"

'I don't think so, but Jon felt it would happen soon.'

"That's why he was always at the spire at sunset."

'Yes.'

"But what does it have to do with us, or the Redlarks?"

'That I can't say for sure. But it seemed he would take this as a sign to return.'

"Are you sure it hasn't already happened? Maybe he's gone!"

'No, I can tell it hasn't come yet.'

"Then I have to be with him when it happens, so I can go with him or at least follow."

I decided I must find Jon and confront him. I didn't tell Raina any of this, not even the part about Feier's telepathy. I wasn't sure she'd understand, and I was probably trying not to get too close to anyone else, either. Something bad seemed to happen to everyone who was close to me. I knew that if I went to the Wilds, I'd leave her behind. But now I realize I should have been more open with her, so she could have chosen for herself. Instead I chose for her, by leaving her out of my plans, and in the end, I lost her when the sign came.

I began to take walks at night, hoping to find Jon somehow. He just seemed to be the kind of person who would walk in the darkness.

[Jon grinned at Jael as he said this. "Do you still think that?" he asked.

"No," Jael laughed, "Not anymore." Then he took a deep breath, and continued.]

One of those nights, it was very foggy. A mist had crept in from the Wilds, and a gray film hung over the world. As I walked, the lights on the street were ghostly halos of glittering gold. The framework of the monorail overhead was lost in the fog. The only hint of its presence was a feeling of size and weight over me. It was uncanny to feel something like that and not see it. Ahead of me, the haze hung in expectant tension, seemingly ready to swirl at any moment. It was as though the world were dead, silent, and yet waiting for something.

Feier was trotting ahead of me quickly and silently, as though he, too, sensed something was about to happen. Then he came back to my side. But neither of us spoke a word, or thought a thought. I felt like nothing but a small bundle of warmth in the midst of a timeless city. I was just one small person against all the powers of Terres.

Intermittent windows sent glows into the air around me. Was that someone watching me, or just my own fears? When I looked around, I saw no shadows.

As I neared the park, there were trees ahead. They cast no ghostly spidery shadows as on other night walks. As I walked beneath them, I listened for my footfalls, but the sound was absorbed in the fog.

Then I suddenly saw a wiry figure ahead of me, and I was sure it was Jon. Just as I saw him, he turned quickly into a narrow alley. I hurried ahead to follow him, Feier close behind me.

In the alley, the walls seemed fuzzy to my eyes and the passage endless. I strained to see something besides gray haze, and listened intently for his footfalls, but only silence came to my ears. The silence was nearly audible, like a dull thud. I began to have strange sensations, like the walls beside me were melting into the mist. I felt that if I touched them, my hand would be swallowed up. All around me was gray silence, no light and no darkness. And no person. Except for Feier, I was alone.

[*"Whew!" Danny let out a sharp breath. "That's scary! What happened then?"*

"Nothing that night," Jael smiled. "But the fog was hiding the secret of what was to come."

"But why did you have all those strange feelings in the alley?" Ginna asked.

"I think it was because of Jon," said Jael, glancing at his companion.

Jon nodded. "That night I finally began to regain my power to make a crossing. It was Jael's first experience with entering the edge of a GAP."

"What about the Sign?" Danny piped in. "Was that it?"

Jon shook his head. "The Sign was soon to come, Daniel. And it was something much more terrible than any of us ever imagined."]

CHAPTER 12

THE DOUBLE STAR

The days began to run together in sameness, *[said Jael]*, until one day I decided to watch the sunset from Neptune Spire again. I hadn't been there or seen Jon anywhere for a long time. Raina didn't want to come with me that day, so I went with Feier.

As I looked down from the top of the spire, everything in the City looked the same. Watching the movement of everyday life below, I began to wonder what made this world the way it was. What would happen if it all suddenly stopped? Would things get better? Would the Council be forced to change the System? Or would things only get worse? I'm not sure why these thoughts came to me. I just had a strange feeling life needed to change, especially for me.

The door from the lift hissed behind me as it opened, and I turned to see Jon. My heart jumped halfway to my mouth.

"Hello, Jon," I said quickly. "How have you been? I haven't seen you for quite awhile."

"Yeah," was his only reply.

He seemed preoccupied and hardly noticed me. Immediately, he took the position he often did, looking toward the Peaks on the far eastern horizon. Did he know something no one else did? Was something about to happen?

Regelian was very low on the horizon now, and shadows of the buildings were lengthening below us. Feier was in my arms, and I was just about to ask him if he knew what Jon was thinking when it came.

A ball of golden fire shot across the darkening sky. I heard a cry and realized it was me. Jon was staring intently ahead and seemed not to hear me. So began one of the strangest events I've ever witnessed.

When I looked to the east, that globe of flame was rushing toward our sun. Then they seemed to meet, but not in the blinding flash I'd expected. Instead, everything became immediately as dark as midnight, with stars overhead. But these stars were whizzing past in unrecognizable patterns. In a matter of minutes, the sun rose in the west and swept across the sky, setting very quickly. Again, it was night, but this time the stars were mere bands of light.

The crazy alternations of day and night continued. Once, as Regelian rose, I saw right beside it a smaller blinding-white star. It looked like our sun was being pulled into another star's gravity, becoming a double star.

These paired suns kept hurtling across the sky, revolving around each other like two tops. The revolutions were so fast that a spiral of flaming gases was trailing after them in space, and I could see sparks raining down on the City. Soon it was dark as night, and I couldn't see what was happening below us.

Nights followed days for what seemed hundreds of sunsets, as gradually the revolutions of suns and planets slowed back to a more normal pace. Again, the double sun set in the east, and this time night came to stay. But as I looked at the stars, they were in totally different patterns than the ones I'd known before. We must have been dragged into a new part of the Galaxy.

When I looked at Jon, he was still standing nearby, staring out with a look in his eyes that seemed to say he'd almost expected all this.

"Did you know this was coming?" I demanded, surprised at my own audacity.

He made no reply, but just pointed at the City below. As I looked down, my heart melted within me. There was a blazing inferno to the south, and it was approaching Neptune Spire at an alarming rate. Then stark terror seized me and I began to scream.

"Raina! She's down there somewhere. I have to find her."

I turned and ran down the ramp, not taking the lift.

Jon was close behind. Just as I reached the ground floor, he caught me and gripped my arm savagely.

"Stop, Jael! It's too late now. The Sign has come, and there's no time left."

I was trembling in spasms of fear, but managed to wrench away and run out into the park.

Out there, everything seemed either black or red. Intact buildings stood starkly against the roaring wall of flame in the south. Screams mingled with the roar, and the heat threatened to knock me over. I ran instead, still crying for Raina. The scenes before me blurred in and out of focus, and I kept wondering if this was another of my terrible nightmares. I almost hoped it was.

Belongings and bodies were strewn across the streets when I emerged from the park. As I started to step over some dark shape, a hand suddenly grabbed me. A woman lying on the pavement pulled me toward her and gasped something that meant nothing to me. Seeing her tortured face sent new spasms of fear through me, and I jerked from her grasp, running again.

I didn't get very far before I came crashing down, tackled from behind. Anger mingled with my terror, and I rolled over ready to bite and scratch. Then I saw Jon, with Feier sitting on his shoulder.

'Please, Jael,' I heard Feier say, 'Listen to Jon. He wants to help.'

"So *now* you think you'll help?" I snapped bitterly. "Have you had a change of heart?"

Just then, voices around us were shouting something about Neptune Spire. Jon was still holding me down, but I raised up enough to see greedy flames leaping at the base of the tower. Its pearly top was glittering as on any starlit night. Then a ripping, crashing sound filled the air, and the pinnacle began to lean. The top was still sparkling as though nothing was happening, right up to the moment the flames engulfed it. Neptune Spire, the pride of Terres, was gone.

I couldn't take anymore. I began to claw at Jon as he sat beside me. This was a bad dream, I screamed, begging him to wake me. Then my strength left me, and I slumped into his arms. He lifted me quickly and began to carry me, moving away from the rapidly approaching flames. Still, the air was extremely hot around us.

Sweat drenched me, and my breath came in labored gasps. Smoke swirled around us, yet Jon kept moving. I began to wonder if he knew where he was going, or was he just in a trance too? I wanted to leave him, to run from this dream and find Raina—my only friend. Perhaps I was stuck in someone else's dream. I began begging that someone to wake up.

Instead I finally fell asleep, a fitful, hot doze at first, then gradually cooler. Cool, wet darkness seemed to pour over me and through me. 'Yes, it was a dream,' I thought. 'Soon I'll wake in my own bed, safe at home.'

***

Jon's voice woke me, speaking strange words, "I will lift up my eyes unto the hills, from whence cometh my help…"

As I sat up slowly, the bright light of day blinded me. I was lying on a pile of dry leaves that crunched and crackled as I moved. Had my dream brought me here?

When my eyes finally focused on Jon, I saw his face was blackened with soot, and his clothes were singed by flames. Looking down at my own clothes, I saw they were just as sooty. Jon's eyes were staring blankly ahead. When I tugged at him, he just sat rigid. I began to wonder if he was dead and I'd only dreamed his words.

Jumping up too fast, I became giddy and leaned against a tree. Then I saw we were on a hilltop overlooking Terres-City. The sight knocked me back down like a physical blow, and I sat staring in disbelief. Everything seemed to be gone—no Neptune Spire, no great buildings or monorail—nothing. I couldn't even cry, but just sat and stared numbly, seemingly past all tears or hope. The new twin sun was shining down on the smoking ruins, and not a thing stirred that I could see. It seemed nothing was left alive there. Only the Wilds were left—and me. Was I truly alone now, more alone than I'd ever been before?

Then I felt a firm hand on my shoulder that caused me to turn in surprise. Steady violet eyes looked right through me, but this time they seemed to be trying to give me some hope.

"Let's go find Martina," Jon said.

I stared up at him, not sure what to think. "You really will take me to her?"

"I'm going back, though I don't know what I'll find. And you don't have anywhere else to go, do you?"

I could only shake my head, looking over the smoldering ruins of the City. "Is there anyone left alive except us?"

"I don't know."

"Maybe I should try to find Raina and Jason."

"You have to choose, Jael—them or Martina. Believe me, it's either the Redlarks or the City—there's no middle ground. If you come with me, you must forget the City altogether. If they do rebuild, they'll forget you. You can never go back."

"But you did."

"Not really. I was no-one in the City. I only learned once and for all that it was not my place."

Silence fell over me as I kept gazing at what had once been my home. I must have sat there for a long time, and Jon didn't speak. I wasn't sure if he understood my thoughts or just had many of his own.

'Perhaps I do have to let go of the past now,' I thought. 'I really have no choice. But there's something inside me that doesn't want to leave.'

Then a soft humming sound brought me out of the depths of thought. Feier was nudging my hand to be petted.

"Feier, where did you come from?" I cried.

'I was scouting ahead for Jon.'

"For Jon!" It made me angry to think of Jon giving orders to Feier.

"He was the only one who could help us here," Jon said evenly. "He did it for both of us. After all, he *is* a creature of the Wilds."

"But he's tame. He's never lived out here."

"He has his instincts, though."

"What?"

"In time, Jael," he added. "Come on now. We can't sit here all day."

I knew then I'd have to wait for answers. Apparently, Jon was the sort who told you things in his own time. But at least I could trust Feier, even if I wasn't so sure about Jon.

"You must have found the lempah," Jon was saying to Feier. More communication between them that bypassed me. But Feier was still sitting in my lap, and I swallowed my anger. He was still mine in the way he'd always been and my only friend now. Even if he was helping Jon, I told myself it was because it also helped me. I'd hold my peace for now. After all, now that Jon saved me from the destruction of the City I probably owed him my life, a great debt, no matter what my personal feelings for him were.

Then Jon took my arm. "You've sat and thought enough, Jael. It's time for action." Well, that wasn't quite an order, but not a question either.

Feier jumped up to follow him, and I pulled myself to my feet. As we entered the first thick trees just over the crest of a hill, I started to take one last look back.

"It's too late to look back now," said Jon.

I had to follow quickly as he and Feier disappeared into the deeper shadows of the forest. I never did get to look back.

After a short walk through the whispering trees, we came to a small glade carpeted with yellow flowers. Scattered among the tiny flowers were shrubs with bright purple berries on them, and here and there a tall tree with velvety brown bark. This opening, Feier told me, was the lempah, the storehouse of the Wilds.

Jon went to work quickly and without a word. First, he pulled long pieces of the brown bark off, and began weaving it in wide strips to form mats. I watched and then tried some myself, surprised that it was harder than he made it look. When I showed him my first attempt, he almost smiled, then began to give me a few pointers on what to do better.

The double sun crossed half the sky while we sat weaving. By then, bark which felt so velvety and soft when we began, started to scratch my hands, and my fingers began to get very dry and sore. When at last Jon indicated we could stop, there were several mats of various shapes and sizes, from the simple coarse ones I made to finer ones Jon did.

Then he began to pull long threads of grass from around him and used them to join the mats together. I watched as his hands seemed to perform magic, turning four coarse mats into a sort of bag that could hang over the shoulder or across the back. A quickly-woven strap of the thread-grass completed it.

"Here," he said, handing it to me. "Use this to gather as many of the berries as it'll hold. Then top it with the tiny green leaves from the saffron-flower plants. We'll spread it all on a rock to dry and make berry leather for the journey."

I nodded, though I wasn't sure what this leather would be like. Perhaps it was something to eat? As I bent over and started to pick berries, he spoke again, "Eat some berries if you're hungry. And Feier can show you where to get a drink of water."

Feier again. But this time I was grateful that he knew, for my throat was feeling parched. The berries tasted good, with a meaty, semi-sweet flavor, and they did take the edge off the hunger that was beginning to gnaw. The sun sank quite low by the time I picked a bagful of berries and leaves.

Jon started to scold me for taking so long, but his voice wasn't really angry.

"We got a late start," I said. "It's not my fault."

To my surprise, he seemed to almost smile at me. "Yes, you're right. We'll just cover them tonight to keep out the frost, and then we can dry them tomorrow. Now come here, you need to be better dressed for the Wilds. These will be much warmer and more comfortable—and they'll last longer, too."

I was astonished to see all he'd done while I picked berries. Where the simple mats had lain were now a large shoulder bag like mine, and two sets of shirts and leggings. There were two blankets rolled to one side, also made of mats sewn together. Jon told me to take off all my clothes. I shivered as I did so, in the beginnings of an early evening breeze.

As I took off my undergarment, something yellow and white fluttered to the ground like a dry leaf. It was my pamphlet. I'd always worn it next to my skin, since the day of the book-burning.

"What's this?" Jon asked, picking it up.

"It's mine!" I cried, suddenly fearful of what he'd do.

"'*Words to Remember*,'" he read from the cover. "What is it, an ancient grammar? The schools don't teach this anymore."

I began to stammer, not even thinking, at first, how strange it was he could read. "It's just from the—I mean—from an old book my family had. I didn't know you could read, too."

"Your family had books?"

"Until someone burned them all. We all could read," my voice faded weakly, as though my heart were in my throat. Was I about to lose my last tiny piece of the past, my home and family?

Jon was turning the little booklet over, looking at it curiously. Then he quoted some more words from the cover, " 'The Lord is my God, my strength, and my song; and now he has become my salvation.' Those are strange words from someone on Terres. What do they mean?"

I shrugged. "My family talked often about God, but I don't understand it all. I hope to someday. That's why I kept this."

My teeth were chattering now, from the combination of the chill wind and my fear. Then relief swept over me as he extended his hand and gave the pamphlet back to me.

"Here," his voice was very thoughtful, "Those words about strength and salvation may help you in the Wilds. You're full of more surprises than I expected. I had no idea anyone on Terres dared to keep ancient books. Your family must have been quite unusual. I admire someone who dares to go against the Council, even in a small way."

I tried to nod a reply, but by this time I was shivering

too much. Jon's eyes were faraway in a sort of reverie. Then suddenly they snapped back and were looking at me again.

"Here, put these on before you freeze." He tossed the smaller pair of clothes to me.

I got into them quickly and felt warm and comfortable almost instantly. They were soft and thick, but not bulky. I felt I could move more easily than in my old clothes, perhaps even more quietly. When Jon put his on, I saw another feature. The color was exactly like the bark of many of the trees, so when he stepped into the forest he seemed to disappear entirely. I knew these were truly the clothes of the Wilds, made from them and for them, and they fit me perfectly. The blanket also seemed to be made especially for me. When I lay on it, the sides curved up and pulled right over me, so I slept cozy and warm in my own sort of sack.

Yet, though I was very tired, the aching of my arms and hands kept me awake for a long time. Or perhaps it was the thoughts haunting my mind. Jon buried my old clothes, and now I had no link left with the City except my pamphlet. There was indeed no looking back now, and who should know that better than Jon?

The stars were twinkling overhead in their strange new patterns. My thoughts burned with them, distant and cold, 'Why did Jon come back to Terres-City if he felt the Redlarks were right? Is there something about Redlarks he fears even more than he hates the City or the Council?

And why is he going back now? Because of the Sign of the double-star? Or because he has no other choice? Do the Redlarks have some power over him that he can't break—that draws him back?'

For an instant, I wanted to jump up and run back to the City. 'There must be someone left there—they will rebuild. I can still live there. There's no need to run away.'

But my new clothes and blanket were too warm to leave. And there was Martina. Didn't I want to find her at any cost? I *had* to go to the Redlarks—it was my only choice. And I had to trust Jon, though in many ways he was still a stranger to me. I'd have to learn to live with my fears, and let each day take care of itself. Perhaps the God of my parents would care for me.

My sleep was fitful most of that night.

A morning mist was just beginning to lift when I woke, but Jon was already up, building a small fire and cooking something he'd snared. I didn't care to even ask what it was—it tasted good, and I was hungry.

We spent most of the day on the berry-leather. First, we pounded the berries and leaves with short, fat pieces of wood. Then the purple paste was re-spread to dry. By evening, it turned to dry leathery strips with the sweet-meaty taste of the berries, mingled with a spiciness from the leaves. We packed these strips into the bags, along with a few fresh fruits and nuts we picked while the leather was drying.

This time, as we lay down to sleep, I knew we'd be starting our journey with the dawn. There was still a knot of fear in my stomach which even food wouldn't ease.

Jon talked more that day as we worked, telling me of dangers I must be careful of in the Wilds—vicious animals, mud bogs, strangling vines, and stinging plants. I didn't fear these things as much as he thought—not nearly as much as I feared something I couldn't even name. But he came close to naming it for me, just as we were drifting off to sleep.

"Jael?"

"Yes."

"Just one more warning."

"There are so many dangers in the Wilds—I know."

"But this one is for you alone, Jael."

I lay silent, my heart pounding.

"I just want you to know that even if we do find your sister, she may be greatly changed, not the Martina you remember at all."

I could think of no reply for him, but just drew Feier closer to me. His warmth and humming soothed me a little, but even he couldn't erase the haunting thoughts in my mind.

When we set off at dawn the next day, I was a strange mixture of feelings. There was the anticipation of what lay ahead, the excitement of at last beginning the journey, and deep inside the nameless fear.

CHAPTER 13

THE WAY IN THE WILDS

It seemed we'd been walking forever. Even in the soft-bark boots Jon made, my feet ached and were covered with blisters. If Jon noticed my limping, he didn't say. He wouldn't consider stopping, except for the night's rest, for many days. There would be too much activity around Terres-City, he said. It would be dangerous to be anywhere nearby. I wasn't sure what he meant.

Once or twice we saw figures at a great distance who seemed to be wearing soft-bark clothes like ours. But I never got a good look at them, for Jon would always pull me down behind a rock or into a thicket as soon as he saw them. I felt sure they were Redlarks—who else could they be? But why did they always seem to be heading *toward* the City? And why did Jon avoid them? It seemed a strange way to return to them—by avoiding them all the time.

The days ran together for me, each one just more plodding through forests and across meadows. It became a sameness of shades of green. In the early days, when I was still more aware, I looked at all the different trees and plants, marveling there were so many kinds. There were more than I'd ever seen in the Park or could have imagined. We could hear flying creatures crying overhead, too, and small creatures scuttling in the underbrush and through tree branches overhead.

Once or twice, there were larger animals grazing or stalking on the open hilltops. But these we saw only from a great distance, and when they sensed our presence, they fled. I wanted to ask Jon questions about all these new and strange sights, but he seemed unwilling to talk much. And soon I was too weary to ask.

["Couldn't you have just crossed the GAP to get there faster?" Danny asked. "Wouldn't that have been easier?"

Jael smiled at this. "I asked Jon that question myself later, when I learned of his power. I'll let him tell you why we didn't."

When they turned to Jon to hear his answer, he had a distant look in his eyes. "There are things we learned on that journey together we wouldn't have learned any other way," he said softly.

"But did you know that in some way before it happened?" asked Ginna.

"No," Jon smiled. "It was planned, but not by me. My only reason then was my power hadn't developed enough for *such a precise journey in the GAP. I had much more to learn first. Making the journey on foot was really the only safe choice we had then."*

Jael was nodding, looking into the honey-colored light of the lamp on the coffee table. He sat for what seemed a long time in silent thought before he resumed.]

It was Feier who kept me going for a long while. Just when I felt I could go no longer, he would lick my hand with his rough tongue or rub against my legs and speak softly in encouraging thoughts. At night when I collapsed into my blanket, he nestled beside me, humming as if crooning me to sleep. The sleep I had those nights was the deep sleep of exhaustion.

Then each morning brought the same meal of dry berry-leather, now tough and tasteless to my tired mouth. The fresh fruits were long since eaten, and more weren't to be found. So, we'd go plodding on again, ever eastward toward those towering Peaks at the edge of the world.

I first began to see the Peaks as the trees were becoming a blur of greens and browns for me. As we topped a ridge, there they were—stark and bare against the sky. But we seemed to get no closer each day, as though they were receding into their haze as we vainly tried to reach them.

But some days, I wasn't sure I wanted to reach those forbidding-looking mountains. Some of the ridges we were crossing were rugged enough for me. The air would grow thin and cold as we labored up the western sides. Vegetation thinned until we were stepping on bare rock. Many a sharp edge cut through the thinning places in my bark-boots, and sometimes right into my feet. The ragged boots became stained dark with blood over most of their soles.

My only comfort was when Feier would lick the wounds for me each night. Something in his saliva must have a pain-reducing property, because it did help. Even Jon seemed concerned for me now, for he'd inspect my feet carefully for signs of infection, saying Feier was indeed a blessing. He never mentioned his own boots were as tattered and stained as mine.

Out of the hazy memories of this time, of the pain and weariness, there is one ridge which stands out to me clearly even now, sharp and cold like a shining knife blade.

It was a knife-edge ridge, with the sharpest rocks we'd encountered. By the time we reached the top, I felt as though I had no soles left on my boots or my feet, and I was close to right. My legs were melting beneath me, and my head was spinning from the heights and thin air. I sank onto a flat rock, and not even Feier could move me on.

"Jael, we can't stay here in full view on such a high point."

"I can't go another step." I gasped.

"You must!"

"Oh, just leave me here to die. That's all I want now."

"Jael, look at me." His voice was commanding, but not angry.

My head lifted slowly, feeling very heavy. Jon was standing close to me, and his violet eyes were gazing deep into mine. Again, I had a strange sensation he was trying to give me something through those eyes, like the day we left the City.

"I know how you feel, Jael, believe me."

Looking down at his feet, I could see they were bleeding too, and despite my weariness I knew his words were true.

"But there are some things about the Wilds you don't know, Little Brother."

I looked up in surprise when he called me that.

But his voice went steadily on, "I know the ways of the Wilds. It's a place where you fight for life or you die. If you sit down on a rock and say, 'I want to die,' you're going to. And if you do that, you'll never find what you're looking for—not your sister or anything else. Now, Jael, nod if you understand."

I nodded, for my voice seemed to be totally gone now.

He was kneeling in front of me, with my arms in his hands. "Now I also understand you're still young, and this is a very hard journey for one so small. You've already lasted longer than I expected. But there's more and rougher country to come, so you must continue to be brave, Little Brother."

There was his new name for me again. Why did those two words make me feel at once warm and yet fearful?

"We will be with you, Feier and I. We won't let you down or leave you to die. So, will you get up now and continue to fight to live?"

Again, I nodded mutely and slowly rose to my feet. As I did, my eyes fell on the Peaks, standing sentinel in the east and bathed in an orange sunset. Did they look a trifle closer now, or was I only wishing it so?

"I will lift my eyes unto the hills, from whence cometh my help…" Jon was saying softly.

"Those strange words," I murmured. "You said them once before, the day we fled the City."

"They're from some ancient book, I'm told," he shrugged. Then his tone changed back to his marching-order voice. "Come on. We've been on top of this ridge in plain view of all the Wilds for too long. And night is coming soon."

As we started down the ridge on its eastern side, the last rays of light were reaching us, and the twin sun was sinking behind the peaks. Soon, it was very dark, and I could barely see where to put my feet.

"I'm afraid I'm going to fall!" I cried.

"I think there's a cave up here," came Jon's voice, from what seemed a great distance.

"Where are you? I can't see!" Fear came rushing at me now in great torrents.

Then came a small voice in my head. 'Listen for me, Jael. I'll hum to you. Come to me.'

"Feier?" I stopped and took a ragged breath, straining my ears to hear him. There it was, out beyond the pounding of my heart, a soft humming, "Come—commm—"

Slowly and as silently as I could, I groped toward that sound. My legs were trembling, and though I could see nothing, I had a sensation of teetering on the edge of a great abyss. Yet, I kept trying to push the raging terror out of my mind, concentrating on that voice, "Comm—"

Then a hand grabbed my arm and pulled. I was so startled I lost all hold on myself and screamed. Great sobs came from my mouth, and tears streamed down my cheeks.

'It's all right, Jael. You're safe with us now,' Feier's thoughts finally worked into my trembling mind.

Rocking, slowly and gently—I realized I was rocking. And warm. These sensations began to sort themselves out in the haze. I was in someone's arms, someone crooning softly. Father? That was my first thought. Perhaps I'd died and was with my father. Or was it Stephen?

Then a voice came—deep and seemingly from a distance, "You're very brave and strong of heart, Jael."

I recognized Jon then. Disbelief flashed across my mind. Jon, holding me, rocking me like a father or a brother? Jon, the task-master, the march-commander? Yet, who else could it be, if I were indeed still alive? My mind strove against a haze seeming to engulf me. I must try to speak to him—to understand this. Must try—must not die—but then I fell asleep.

***

The sleep washed back from me slowly, like an ebbing tide. I became aware of orange light and then moving shadows on rough rock walls. Turning my head, I saw Jon, squatting by a small fire he was tending. Feier sat beside him, his eyes reflecting the light.

"Do you feel better now?" came Jon's voice. He hadn't even looked over at me. Then I realized Feier must have told him I was awake.

I rose gingerly to a sitting position. "I'm hungry," I muttered.

"Come by the fire, where it's warmer. I've tried to fix something that will give you strength."

As I moved toward him, I was surprised at how weak and shaky I felt. I sat down quickly beside Jon, trying to hide this. He handed me a rough sort of bowl with some steaming liquid in it. As I sipped it, I could feel some strength beginning to return, spreading through me slowly with the warmth. It tasted like berry-leather boiled in water, but there was another flavor in it. Could it be meat? I didn't put the bowl down until I'd drunk it all.

"Not too bad, huh?" said Jon.

"It *was* good."

We sat in silence then. He seemed more his old self again, sitting at a little distance from me, with Feier between us. It was hard to believe he'd really held me and rocked me to sleep. Or had it only been a delirious dream? I tried to think of something to say to him, but each time I tried, the words flowed back out of my mind like water through my hands. I could barely think for more than an instant. So it was Jon himself who finally broke the silence:

"Get out your little book, why don't you? Perhaps it has some words of strength for us."

Digging deep inside my shirt, I pulled out the frayed pamphlet. It fell open of itself, and my eyes slowly focused on the words. Then I felt a sudden shock. Was I still in some strange dream? I'd never known these words were in this book, but here they were:

"I will lift up my eyes unto the hills, from whence cometh my help," I dimly heard my voice reading.

"My song!" Jon cried suddenly, moving closer to me. "How did you get that?"

"It's just here," I said, my mind whirling. "The words of this pamphlet are from The Book."

"The book? What book?"

"That's all it's ever called. My family read from it every night."

"But what book? What's it about?" His voice sounded urgent now.

"I don't know. I was too young to understand much then. All I know is it talked about God—the Lord who made Earth and Heaven."

He was looking at the words with me now, in stunned silence. His eyes then stared into the fire, and he seemed to be off in one of his reveries again.

"It's my song," his voice came quietly, sounding far away. "I can remember my mother singing it to me as a child. Then Amian, the Redlark, sang it to me, and I thought it was true that my help lay with them, at the foot of the Peaks. But now I wonder."

These words made me shiver. What did he mean? It was as though he was torn about whether to go back to the Redlarks or not. What happened to him there? Why had his words of hope from The Book become words of question? Then my eyes fell on the page in my hand again. The rest of the words seemed to leap out at me:

'My help cometh from the Lord.'

I pulled at Jon's sleeve. "Look, there's more to the verse than what you've said. Did you know that?"

He seemed to pull himself back from a great distance. "What?"

"Listen," I said. "It says more. 'I will lift up my eyes unto the hills; from whence cometh my help? My help cometh from the Lord, who made heaven and earth.' It doesn't say your help comes from the hills; it says it comes from the Lord."

"But how can it come from some Lord that I don't even understand?"

"I don't know. But the hills must be important, too, or they wouldn't be in the verse. Perhaps it means we'll find help from God when we look to the hills."

"Perhaps." His voice was full of doubt, but there was an undertone which seemed to say he wanted to believe me.

Slowly his arm reached out and touched my shoulder. I felt completely natural leaning against him. It was good to be sheltered at last.

"Maybe we'll understand when we reach the Peaks," I said softly.

"I hope you're right, Little Brother."

"Jon?"

"Hunh?"

"Why do you call me that—Little Brother?"

"I guess because I can sense your need for a big brother," he murmured, brushing my hair back from my eyes. "You really miss them, don't you?"

"Especially Stephen. He was almost a father to me, after Father died in the wars."

Then we were silent for a long time. I could feel him breathing deeply, evenly. Just when I'd decided to myself he had nothing else to say, he added, "I never had a brother. But if I did, I'd want him to be like you."

I couldn't think of any reply to this, so I just snuggled against him, glad of the chance to feel peaceful for once. 'Just to rest,' my mind said softly. 'That's all I need.'

For I knew we'd be off again with the light of morning.

CHAPTER 14

RIVERS RUNNING DEEP

If I'd known what lay below us on the east side of the ridge, I might never have left that cave. The terrain was even steeper than the western side. There was no vegetation, and the rocks were crusted in places with snow and ice. I hadn't often seen these cold, white forms of water, but they held no fascination for me now. They were treacherous, as Jon patiently coaxed and guided me over the sharp and slippery precipices.

Then as we went lower, the air warmed slightly, and the ice began melting, sending cold trickles down the rocks. These tiny streams merged to waterfalls, which crossed directly into our path. Here again, Jon coached and lifted me through the icy waters. Sometimes, he slung me over his back as he crept carefully down the cliffs.

When we finally reached some vegetation and gentler slopes, I was still riding on his back, my cheek resting on his shoulder. He made no motion to put me down, though I'm sure I was heavy. Soon I was half-dozing in and out of sleep, as we swung along through rolling terrain and a blur of green forest.

I'm not sure how long I slept in sheer exhaustion. I was lying in one of those lempah-glades when I woke. For an instant, I wondered if we were back at the first glade and I'd dreamed the whole journey. But the sound of voices soon told me otherwise.

"You aren't Redlarks, in spite of your clothes," one was saying.

"Only a clever disguise, don't you think, Carn?" came another.

"Let me do the talking, Thel! You only state the obvious."

Then I heard the welcome sound of Jon's voice, "We're seeking the Redlarks—to join them."

"Perhaps you're spies from Terres-City? You have the reek of the City about you," came the rough voice called Carn. I kept my eyes tightly closed, pretending to still be asleep.

"That one's young to join the Redlarks," piped in Thel's higher-pitched voice again. I knew he meant me.

"I told you to shut up!" Carn cried, and there was the sound of a loud slap.

"OW! All right, all right!"

I could hear Thel move closer to me, away from the others. Then Jon's voice came, still very even and steady, "He escaped the destruction of the City with me."

"Destruction!" squeaked Thel.

"Thel!" Carn roared. Then with an ominous suddenness, his voice was low again, questioning Jon, "So you *have* been in the City within the moon? And how am I to know they haven't sent you to spy?"

"There's no one left in charge to send spies," Jon replied coolly. "And my knowing of the City's destruction doesn't brand us either. We've seen your raiding parties on their way toward the city to loot and pillage."

"Enough!"

"Oh, is that a secret? Your people were too easy to see, if that's the case."

"Maybe I should kill you both and have done with it," Carn rumbled.

"But perhaps your High Chieftain will feel cheated out of his judgment."

"He's right," Thel said quickly. "Rigan would be furious with us."

Suddenly there was a crash as if something was thrown at Thel. It landed very close to my head, and I sat up suddenly in spite of myself.

Jon moved quickly to my side in the confusion. "Don't speak!" he hissed in my ear.

He kept his body close to mine as a shield while Carn

and Thel scuffled. For an instant, it looked as though Jon planned to make a run for it, but then the bout ended suddenly, with Thel rubbing his head and sulking under a tree.

Then Carn gave a shrill whistle like we'd heard flying creatures make in the forest. Four more bark-clothed figures appeared as if from nowhere.

"Get these captives moving," Carn ordered. "We'll let the High Chieftain dispose of them as *he* pleases."

Jon was grabbed roughly by a nearby figure, but he shrugged the hands off. Then he got up under his own power and picked me up gently. "It's okay, Jael," he whispered as we started through the trees. "You've come this far bravely. Don't let go of your fight to live now. This is just one more of the ways of the Wilds."

It seemed we marched a long way, though the time is lost to me. My mind was cloudy and my bones ached. Jon carried me most of the time, as the marchers were too fast for me to keep up on my own. I often dozed in his arms or on his back. Once I lay half-awake thinking he was Stephen, before I finally remembered this was impossible. I do remember beginning to feel a sort of kinship with Jon, after all we'd been through together. I was glad I was with him as we went to the chieftain's camp, for it would have been impossible for me to make this trip alone.

In fact, I must have lost consciousness at some point, because there's a period of blackness when I remember nothing at all. My memory returns with the sound of rushing water and a rocking motion beneath me.

"Where am I?" a voice cried from within me.

"Sh! Jael. It's okay. We're on the river." I knew this was Jon. With a piece of cloth in his hand, he was wiping my forehead and brushing back my hair.

"Your fever has broken," he said softly. "That's good. Welcome back to the world."

Then I saw him give me the first real smile I'd ever seen. I tried to smile back, but it was a feeble attempt. Still, it was good to see the worry lines on his brow smooth and fade away. I tried to sit up, and found I was tightly wrapped in a blanket.

"Just lie still for awhile yet," he said. "The river will be with us for a long time."

I must have slept again. The next time I woke, I was feeling much stronger, and Jon propped me up in the blanket. I was glad to see Feier sitting beside me, smiling.

We were in the center of a long, narrow boat made of wood and bark. Six men were paddling, three in front of us, and three behind. Another man in the rear of the boat was standing and using a long oar to steer. I'd never seen a boat before, much less been on water, so every move they made was fascinating.

When I finally turned my attention to the river itself, I saw a wide body of smooth-looking water. Green banks, thickly forested, were on either side, but ahead was a continuing ribbon of gently-flowing silver. Sometimes a wind ruffled the surface and then it sparkled and danced. I leaned on Jon's shoulder and whispered to him, "It sure is beautiful."

"It was worth the fight to stay alive, huh?" he said softly.

The days continued to roll along, but now I was aware again. The river, I discovered, had many faces. On some days, it was the smooth silvery expanse I'd first seen. But sometimes the winds beat on us hard, and waves rose as high as the great curved prow of our boat.

Periodically, the river tossed itself into froth and foam as it tumbled over rocks and falls. Some of these rapids we shot through, the spray flying and my breath leaving me. Other times, the boatmen by-passed the rapids, beaching the craft and carrying it and all the gear around the falls. Each of the 'carrys,' as they called them, had well-worn paths to walk on.

But for me the most amazing thought was these beautiful and exciting sights were out here in the Wilds all along, and I'd missed them, thinking I was content with the little parks in Terres-City. I was almost glad for the chain of events that forced me out to see all this.

One day, we reached a point where another river flowed into ours. Here the boat was turned and headed upstream into the new, smaller stream. The going was rougher against the current, I discovered. In places where the flow was especially strong, all the men except the steersman in the back took a rope tied to the thwarts and pulled from the shore, inching us upstream. It was very slow, but we would've made no progress paddling. When the going was roughest, they forced Jon to help. As I watched him, I could tell he had great strength in his lean frame. The Redlarks seemed surprised at this, too.

For awhile, the forest closed in on us, as the river got narrower and steeper in its bed. Then one day, there was a large meadow on either side, with the river meandering gently through it, in great sweeping curves. But the greatest surprise was when I looked upward to my right. There were peaks looming right over us. They looked so close I almost felt they might fall on us at any moment. As I looked more closely, I recognized the shapes of some of the crags. These were the Peaks I'd seen so often before, the Peaks at the edge of the world. Now I was at their very base, so I must be at the edge of the world myself.

I strained my eyes to see features on the rocky faces, but only great crags of gray rock, dotted with shining white snow, met my gaze. Below were some rolling green foothills, and at the base of these I could see what looked like small bark mounds scattered across the meadow.

"There's the chieftain's camp," Jon whispered to me.

As we drew closer, I saw columns of smoke rising from holes in the tops of the mounds. These must be some sort of dwelling. Soon I saw they were built of wood and thatch, held together with mud. Colors of reds, blues, and yellows began to emerge from the blur of green and brown as we got close enough to make out the shapes of people. In spite of myself, my heart began to race in anticipation, thinking Martina might be in this very camp.

There was a great commotion and many shouting voices as we beached the boat, and Jon and I were led up into the center of the camp. After so many days in the Wilds, and with the aftermath of the fever, the noise was ear-splitting to me. I was in a daze and very glad of Feier on my shoulder and Jon's hand on my arm, keeping me steady on my feet.

Then amid the tumult, I saw my sister where I least expected. She was up on a dais, seated right beside a brightly-dressed man who must be the High Chieftain. Her dark hair was flowing down and interwoven with flowers and pieces of shell. A cry escaped me, and Jon gripped me tightly.

"There's Martina!" I gasped. "Right up there—beside him."

"Sh! You mustn't speak to the High Chieftain or his Consort."

"But Jon, she's my sister!"

Just then I saw her look down at us, but her eyes went past me and stopped at Jon. "What are these rabble, Carn?" she asked, her voice as cold as a steel knife cutting my heart. She didn't even seem to recognize me!

"I tried to warn you," Jon's voice came softly from somewhere.

"What is the judgment of the High Chieftain Rigan and the fair Indril on these two wanderers?" Carn's voice boomed.

"They've come from the City?" came the cold tone of Rigan.

"Yes, they claim to have fled its destruction."

Rigan frowned, looking hard at Jon. It was almost as though he saw something he recognized and didn't know what to think. "I'll hand this judgment to Indril," he nodded to the one beside him.

Martina stood and I could see her body was as strong and finely-formed as ever. I wanted to run to her, to somehow make her see me, but Feier's claws dug deep into me every time I squirmed, and Jon was gripping my arm fiercely.

"In these days," her voice was saying, in a tone I barely recognized, "We must be more than careful. The Sign has warned us. They're of no use to us now that the City is gone. Therefore, I Indril, pass the judgment of elimination. They will be killed immediately."

My head was spinning. My own sister, condemning me to die, after I'd nearly perished searching for her! A great cry welled up in me, "Mar-!"

Jon cut it off with his hand thrown over my mouth. I bit hard.

CHAPTER 15

A TIME OF DARKNESS

"Is this the judgment you would pass on Jonah, your High Chieftain?" I stood in shock as Jon's voice rang out. "Will you listen to this usurper Rigan and his uninitiated Consort? Rigan was only to reign in my stead, while I returned to the City seeking the Sign. Now I've returned, the Sign is in the sky, and I've brought these Children of the Sign through great perils in the Wilds. Have I brought you this great gift only to have it tossed aside by this one who fears to speak," he pointed an accusing finger at Rigan, "and this one who knows nothing?"

Martina looked very angry as he referred to her this way, and started to rise to her feet. Jon continued quickly and left her standing with her mouth open. "I choose to think she was kept from the truth by no fault of her own. Rigan always likes to keep his women in darkness. So now, Rigan! Tell us *your* judgment, which is what was asked for."

As Jon's voice cried so strongly beside me, chills were

running all through me. I could see now where he'd gotten his ability to speak so well when he needed to, how he had such strong words for me when I sat on a rock wanting to die. I could also tell there was much about him and his journeys that I didn't know or understand. Was it true, as he now said, that he'd planned to come back all along? Or had he just made this up to try to save us?

Thoughts like these were flashing through my mind like bolts of lightning, even as he spoke. And there was much stirring and murmuring in the crowd around us. Voices were whispering, "Jonah? Is it truly him?"

One voice that sounded like Thel's was calling loudly, "It *is* Jonah!" I knew there was something about him. I just knew it!"

Rigan was standing beside Martina now, his face contorted and his fists clenched tightly. When Jon finished, he shouted, "So you claim to be Jonah? And am I to just believe you and step down from my hard-won throne? You have no proof you aren't some clever spy. I stand by Indril's judgment!"

My heart sank. Then voices rang out near us, "Prove yourself, Jonah! If you can defeat him, we'll accept you!"

Then one very hard-sounding voice, which I believe was Carn's, came above the rest, "Force him to the Duel, Rigan. For only the strongest should be High Chieftain."

Other voices were joining him, "Yes! The Duel! It's the only way to know."

Jon was looking straight at Rigan, whose face was very hard and angry. "*Do you* accept my challenge, Rigan?"

"I accept—stranger."

Cries for Jonah, and others for Rigan, were beginning to rise around us. The crowd was parting, leaving a large open circle. As they moved, Jon took me with him to the right of the dais. I was still holding Feier tightly. Rigan was just stepping down, stripped to the waist, as Jon took off his shirt. He started to say, "Jael, if I..."

"I know. If you lose, it will be the end of my journey, too."

"Yes. But what I mean to say is, if I win you may not like that either. Just try to understand. We have no choice now but to live as Redlarks."

I nodded, afraid to speak and hear my voice crack with fear. What did he mean? Then he left me and walked into the open ring. Someone handed him a horrible-looking hooked blade which he swung over his head. A terrible animal-like cry came from his throat, and Rigan answered. I was watching Jon, who'd always seemed so quiet, become a wild beast before my eyes.

For much of the fight I clutched Feier and buried my face in his fur, afraid to watch. From furtive glances, I knew they were leaping at each other, and the jagged curved blades flashed in the sun, seemingly forever. Then came a piercing cry, more high-pitched than the first ones, and the awful sound of a blade entering flesh. My eyes opened against my will. One figure was silhouetted against the sky, blade overhead, bringing it down with tremendous force. The figure on the ground writhed and then was still. I was afraid to look at who stepped back, wiping blood from his blade. I knew who it was when the cries began:

"Jonah! Long live Jonah! High Chieftain!"

Then I looked and saw a fierce fire in Jon's eyes that I'd never seen before and hoped I'd never see again.

"And now," Jon cried, "I take Indril…"

For an instant, I was afraid he would kill her, too.

"…as *my* Consort!"

She rose obediently on the dais and stood in silence, looking steadily at Jon. The sun made some of the shells in her hair flash, and the long dark tresses shone. I realized for the first time she was beautiful, but she was also a total stranger to me now.

Then the look on Jon's face made me shudder—the wild animal was still there. As they stood gazing at each other, electricity seemed to flow between them, reminding me of times I'd seen her with Jason. A tight angry knot began to form in my stomach, though I wasn't sure why.

Then a figure stepped in front of me, blocking the sight.

"Child of the Sign," said a soft voice. "I'm to care for you."

I looked up into a young feminine face that was smooth and calm. She almost seemed to be in a trance.

How could she be so calm amid the charged atmosphere all around us?

"Who told you to take care of me?" I asked suspiciously.

"Your friend here," she patted Feier's head.

"He can talk to you, too?"

"When he wishes to. Come now, you're too young for all this." She tossed her head, and I knew she meant what was happening in the circle. "You have much to be taught."

As we rose and started away from the circle, I glanced toward the dais out of the corner of my eye. Jon and Martina were standing close now, their lips pressed together and his hand tight across her back. I clutched Feier and turned to follow the young woman.

After winding along a path through small trees, we stopped at one of the huts, and she crawled inside. I set Feier down, and he followed, so I went in after him, feeling that at least he wouldn't betray me. Inside, the light was dim and the air smoky from a small fire burning beneath a hole in the roof.

"You must be hungry," she said, handing me a bone with some meat hanging on it.

I took it without a word and began gnawing. It tasted very good after weeks of dry berry-leather.

"My name is Daiah. It's a word from an ancient language that means compassion."

I looked up and noticed her voice and face seemed to fit her name.

"My name is Jael, but I don't know what it means."

"That's your City name. You can't use it here. We must give you a new one." She paused in thought. "I know! You're Stel, which means star. For you came with the new star."

"New star?"

"The double-star."

Then I knew she meant our new sun.

After I'd eaten, she helped me get my ragged boots and shirt off, and rolled me in a soft blanket.

"You should sleep now, Stel." Her voice was very soft, and she was stroking my hair back from my forehead. Her touch was unlike a mother's or a sister's, or anyone else I'd ever known. I wasn't sure what it all meant. "When you're stronger, Stel, we'll begin your teaching."

As I closed my eyes, I felt very strange. There was kindness—yes, and compassion—in her voice. But there was something else I couldn't grasp that brought back my knot of fear.

***

The days began to flow together for me again. There was green sunlight through trees on bright days, and sometimes the dancing light of waves on water. And there were gray days with rain pattering on the roof as we huddled by the fire to keep warm.

I was with Daiah all the time, and I didn't see Jon or my sister for many days. When we went hunting in the forest, stalking small animals quietly with a short spear, Daiah told me how to obey the spirits of the trees, the rocks, and the animals. When she taught me how to paddle a small boat on the river, she told me how to listen to the spirits of the wind and the water.

The days were good for the most part, especially when the warm sun shone. I learned quickly and showed some skill, especially on the river. Daiah liked to call me "Stel, the Waterman." But deep inside I knew something was wrong. My fear receded to a hollow space deep inside me, but that space was like a darkness within which was slowly growing.

Eventually I did see the Chieftain and his Consort a few times. Martina, or Indril, still showed no signs of recognizing me. And now that Jon was High Chieftain, he seemed to want nothing to do with me. I was with Daiah on the fringes of the camp, so I seldom saw them. Jon acted as though I wasn't supposed to recognize him as Jon, but only as Chieftain. I began to wonder if he, too, had forgotten me. Perhaps forgetting all your past was part of being a Redlark, but if this was true, why did I still remember them and the rest of my family? This only caused the empty, dark space inside me to grow more.

My chief consolation was Feier. He seemed to take to wild-life even more than I, and he was an especially good hunter. I didn't have to give him any of my food, for he caught his own. And he was talking more to me now in my mind—telling of things he could see close to the ground that I couldn't, and of things he heard which I didn't. So, the bond between us became stronger each day.

Daiah must have noticed this, for one day she asked, "How did you find your feier-cat?"

"He was a gift from Raina, my friend." My voice suddenly cracked. I hadn't said Raina's name since we left the City but I'd thought of her often.

"She must have been a very dear friend."

I nodded. "I really miss her."

***

One day it was very cold and gray, but instead of rain, snow fell from the sky, covering the ground in white. As we huddled close to the fire for warmth, Daiah began to speak of the spirits of the body, and what they asked of us.

"The spirits within are like any other," she said softly, "the tree-spirits or the water-spirits. We must obey and do what they tell us. It's the Way of the Wilds. When Jonah defeated Rigan and took Indril, he was merely obeying the spirits within him."

I didn't like the sound of this, remembering the wild animal look in Jon's eyes that day. Though Daish's words about these spirits sounded simple enough, there was something making me feel uncomfortable. As I sat silently, trying to think of something to say, she moved closer to me and took my hand in hers.

"Like now," she whispered, "My spirit is telling me to take you and kiss you."

I wanted to ask her what it meant when two spirits told me conflicting things—as they were now. But I had no chance to ask, for she pulled me to her and held me tightly as her lips searched for mine.

"I could teach you so much," she breathed in my ear.

Why was my heart pounding so hard? Then her lips were on mine again—soft and warm—caressing. This was like nothing I ever felt before. Her embrace seemed to engulf me.

But then a voice in my mind said, 'You don't have to do this.' I don't know if it was Feier who spoke or some spirit. But suddenly I broke out in a cold sweat, and fear rippled through me. Tearing myself from her embrace, I stumbled through the door and out into the snow.

Her voice followed me, calling for me to wait, but I turned and ran as fast as I could in the heavy, wet snow. The air was biting cold as I ran, and with each breath my chest ached. I hoped the air would clear my head, but it kept on spinning. The whites and browns of the woods around me whirled and flashed. Then suddenly I came crashing to the ground, lying stunned and wet in the snow.

A crackling sound behind roused me, and then Daiah

was at my side, helping me up. "I'm sorry, Stel," she said. "There's no need to be afraid. The spirits within don't mean to harm us. Please come back."

I shook my head, trying to hide my tears.

"Why are you crying?" she asked.

"What does it mean when two spirits tell me opposite things—one says I should do something, and one says I shouldn't?"

"You must listen to the strongest spirit."

"Then I can't come back," I said.

She looked very surprised at this, and sat down on a nearby log. Then she spoke again, shaking her head, "I've never met one of you. Oh, I didn't mean—well, I don't know!"

"What? Daiah, whatever are you talking about?"

"You must be one of the Chosen." Her voice suddenly had a strange note of reverence in it, and her eyes glowed at me. "The Chosen are set apart from the body—for the Magic."

"The Magic?"

"Yes. We mustn't delay. Tomorrow I'll take you to the High Priest."

Then she took my hand and led me back to her hut, but her touch was very different this time, almost as though she were afraid of me. For the rest of the day, we talked little, and no more was said about the spirits of the body.

So Daiah took me to the High Priest the next day, through a bright sunshine that was melting the snow. First, however, she said we must prepare ourselves, sitting beside a small tallow candle set in the center of her hut.

We didn't say anything. "It's silent contemplation", she said. Then she wove strings of shell pieces into my hair, which was long enough by now to braid.

I felt very strange, but there was even more to come. She sewed pieces of bone and shell to my tunic, so I made rustling and jingling sounds whenever I moved.

"I sure won't be able to hunt in this tunic anymore," I told her, but she only smiled.

Then came the last piece of my new outfit, a wreath woven of dried flowers with a pearly white shell dangling on one side. With great solemnity, she put this on my head, and I heard the shell tinkling like a bell. I felt quite foolish, but she was chanting soft and low.

I caught a few of the words, "Serve the Spirit of The People well, O Stel, Child of the Sign, Son of the Double-star, Chosen of the Great Ones—Chosen One."

This ritual was all very foreign to me, after growing up in the technology and cool objectivity of Terres-City. But despite my own doubts, there was a response somewhere deep inside me, rising as though something long-repressed in me was at last awakening.

These feelings continued, but began to mingle with fear when we arrived at the great tent of the High Priest.

The ceilings in this lodge were high, so no one had to stoop on entering. On the far wall were thick plush-looking hangings, hinting at more beyond them.

The Priest was sitting on cushions below these curtains, flanked by an assistant on either side. All three were dressed in long, dark robes that fell around them in great folds. I could tell the High Priest from the others by the headdress he wore, covered with feathers of many assorted colors. Darkness crept around that place and everything seemed mysterious. My heart felt dark and still, wondering what lay ahead for me.

Suddenly a voice boomed, though I don't remember seeing anyone's lips move, "Who seeks audience with the Priest of The People?"

Daiah suddenly seemed very frightened and pushed me forward ahead of her. The three looked over my strange new outfit, but I think their surprise was at my small size, not the tunic and wreath.

"Speak!" boomed the voice again.

"L-lord, Most High, our P-priest, this is Stel, Child of the Sign, Son of the Double-star. I've found him to be one of the Chosen."

For the first time, I saw some movement on the High Priest's face—he raised an eyebrow. Then there was a rustle, and one of the assistants rose. He pulled Daiah aside and asked her several questions, to which she nodded furiously, talking in quivering whispers. Then he turned and nodded to the High Priest.

"You may go!" the bodiless voice boomed.

The assistant moved Daiah quickly to the door. She didn't look back at me, but stumbled into the sunlight, turned and ran. I wondered if I'd ever see her again. She'd left me to the next stage of my fate. And as I stood before those three dark figures, I had a feeling the end of the darkness inside me was nowhere in sight.

CHAPTER 16

THE DARKNESS DEEPENS

["Why did all the Redlarks change their names?" asked Danny.

"I think it was because they were supposed to forget their pasts, right?" Ginna said.

"That's part of it," Jon replied. "Also, many of them forgot everything because of the drugs and spirit trances they used."

"And we weren't supposed to remember where we came from," added Jael.

"It seems sort of scary," said Danny.

"Well, it was," Jael admitted. "And it had strange effects on some people, especially my sister Martina."

"Fortunately, Jael wasn't affected in the same way. He was much stronger than most of us," Jon smiled.

Jael's face flushed in embarrassment. "Well, you remembered your past, too, Jon. And it was a good thing you did."

"We'd better get on with the story, Jael."

"Okay."]

My internship for the priesthood wasn't so bad at first. The High Priest sent one of his assistants, who took me to the room which was to be my own. He said, "You must study and prepare. There's much to learn before you'll be ready for the rites and ceremonies. Then we'll know if you're truly Chosen."

Apparently, I was being tested. He bowed out the door, leaving me to look around the room, wondering what my fate would be.

The room was full of books, shelves of them lining three walls. I'd never seen so many books in one place before, and I felt it would take me a lifetime to read every one. The assistant, Jah had indicated where I should start, with one called *Patterns of Truth and Life*. "This one," he said, "Is the key to all the rest."

But he didn't have to encourage me to read, for I was hungry to devour every book I could get my hands on.

I didn't feel lonely, with the companionship of the books and Feier. He seemed to want to talk a great deal about what I read. So together we learned, and thought— then talked, and thus learned more. I spent so much time in pursuits of the mind and soul I hardly remembered to feed my body, except when Jah or one of the Temple Maidens brought a meal.

There was so much to learn! My mind would soar on wings of new ideas, and reach out to grasp the next concept before the book's writer did. Sometimes the connection between one idea and another would suddenly emerge like a bright flash of light, as though a mental circuit was completed.

Yet when I try to remember these ideas now, it's difficult. I can recall the thrill of discovery better than the things discovered. Perhaps that was the only real value of this time, the process itself. Still, I'll try to describe some of these ideas, for the sake of showing how naïve I was then, though I didn't realize it at the time.

The first book told the story of how the star-pioneers left Earth to settle new worlds. I began to realize those tales Martina told me long ago might be true after all. But there was one big difference from her stories. While this book on 'patterns' said the first settlers on Terres had indeed come from Old Earth, it also said now we'd 'come of age,' and it was time to shrug off the 'tyranny' of the King of Heaven and Earth and his distant rule. Instead, we could be our own people now, '*The People*' as the Redlarks called themselves.

I was confused by all this. In my world of Terres-City, there were those who followed The Council, and on the other side, people like my parents and brothers who said they were loyal to this King of Heaven and Earth. But here in the Wilds, was a group who seemed opposed to both of these forces.

This Earth King, the book continued, was *not* at one with the Great Spirit, the power of the Universe. This was the direct opposite of what my family taught. Instead, The People were dedicated to helping each person find their own Spirit Within, so each could be true to him or herself.

So, was this Great Spirit of the Universe the *God* my parents had talked of, or not? How could I find out?

The book also said each of us must climb to higher levels of spiritual progression. Our bodies would fall away eventually, but the spirit or soul went to the next level and received a new body. If I lived well enough, my spirit would rise to a higher level. If not, my spirit would descend to a lower level.

I looked at the drawings in this book long and hard. One was of a staircase that seemed to become narrower as it ascended. Apparently, few souls reached the highest level, where spirit was lost and merged with the Great Spirit, at last. I liked to think of finally being at one with the power of the Universe—how much I'd be able to understand then, things I couldn't understand now. And I liked to think of Stephen or my father living a new life somewhere in a higher body.

But then Feier began, as he often did, to ask me questions, 'How is this any different from what they taught us in the City about separation of the mind and body?'

I had no good reply for him, but I tried, "Well, they both put the mind and body separate from each other. But that's all the similarity I see."

'Think of it this way,' Feier insisted, 'Perhaps these

People are only a natural outgrowth of Terres-City, not a real change or alternative.'

"You mean they're basically the same, though they claim to be so different?" I didn't want to believe this. I'd left my whole life to follow Jon, hoping I'd find something better, something closer to what my family taught. I was angry with Feier for putting holes in my new-found answers.

'You should look at things more deeply,' Feier continued. 'For example, if all depends on how you live, good or bad, who decides or judges this?'

Now I was really confused. "The Priests? Or perhaps I can judge for myself?"

'How can a person judge themselves?' he continued. 'No one can truly judge himself without bias. Don't you just make allowances for yourself?'

"Well, I guess I probably do. After all, I'm not perfect."

'That's exactly what I mean.'

He'd let me talk myself right into a corner. I found myself trying to change the subject. "Perhaps I'll be perfect someday."

'After you've worked your way up this supposed stairway? How many lives do you think it will take—a hundred, a thousand?'

My throat tightened at the thought of this. I saw in my mind an endless succession of lives, each trying so hard to be better than the last. And it suddenly struck me as so futile. How would I know, with each and every action or thought of my life, which was the good, and which the bad? Would one wrong decision cause me to go lower rather than higher? I knew I'd probably made some wrong decisions without even realizing it. Was it already too late? My heart began to fill with darkness again.

'And what is this highest level they seek?' Feier continued. 'What is the reward of all your agony and effort?'

"To be at one with the Great Spirit of the Universe." My heart lifted at this thought, until Feier spoke again:

'But what does this mean? To completely lose yourself in the power and presence of this Spirit? Then you'll cease to be yourself, to be Jael. You'll lose all the awareness you worked so hard to gain in life. You won't even know who you are, let alone where you are. Will you even *be*?'

Nothingness. Such a great unfathomable thing! This left me speechless. And angry. It seemed the beauty I thought I'd found in these novel ideas was fading and falling around me like dying flowers.

"Just go away!" I shouted at Feier. "You keep ruining my thoughts with questions. I *need* to know this Great Spirit—somehow I know he's real."

'Oh yes, God is real. That's why you feel this in your heart. And you will find a way to him someday. But please read other books besides these, and don't jump at an idea until you've tested it. Everything must be examined carefully.'

I still felt hurt and angry with him. But when he started out the door, I called, "You *will* return, won't you?"

'Of course I will, but right now I must talk to Jon.'

Jon? What did he have to say to Jon, who'd seemingly abandoned me to empty thoughts and confusion of spirit? Feier was gone before I could ask him.

I tried to go back to the book I was reading, but so many doubts and questions kept coming into my mind, 'How can I ever be perfect, always do the right thing? Am I destined to go ever downward, living lives of futility without end? And if I ever do go upward and reach the top, is it worth gaining, anyway?'

At last I threw the book into the wall and left it lying open, then stalked out the door into the camp.

No spirits, from the forest or within myself, spoke to me that day. Everything was silent. But my eyes were wide open, somehow, with a keen awareness. I saw people around me arguing with each other. I saw men drawing women who weren't their mates into their huts. The darkness of wrong seemed to be everywhere, right here in the very People who claimed to be better, to be reaching for 'higher things.'

Then I saw one of the Temple Maidens slipping into the High Priest's hut. Soon the all-too familiar sound of love-making could be heard. The idea of the Chosen Ones—those set apart from the body to serve the higher spirits only—was just a lie. Perhaps Daiah, in her innocence, honestly believed in the Chosen, but now I saw it was just another falsehood. A great anger and blackness rose in me then. Was there any place where the truth existed?

I was leaning against a gnarled tree, staring vacantly into the air when Jah found me. For a moment, I didn't want to tell him anything of my black mood, but in spite of myself, angry words came spilling out, "How can I know if any of this is true and not a pack of lies?" I cried.

"What do you mean?" he asked.

"Well, all this stuff about each life coming back as something better or worse? Who's to say what's good or bad? Who can judge?"

"We try to judge for ourselves," he said calmly.

"You mean we try to make excuses for ourselves." I wanted to put my fist into his mouth, but knew it wouldn't help. "There has to be someone or something beyond us to judge. Otherwise we're just fooling ourselves."

At this, he just shrugged. "I think you have enough of books and thought now. It's time for the Rituals to begin."

He took my arm then, and pulled me along with him. At first, I thought about resisting, but decided it was futile at this point. So, he took me a great distance to the base of the mountains, to a place where many different trees grew. He carried a clear piece of stone, which he gazed into periodically. At last, we stopped beside a very tall gnarled tree, with pale green branches which drooped until they almost touched the ground.

"This is your special tree, Stel," he chanted. "The crystal has shown it. The spirit of your tree will be your guide in the Ritual Journey. It will show you the truth of the Forest Spirits." He pulled some of the leaves from one of the low-hanging branches and put them in a small bark bag he carried.

Looking around carefully, I noticed all the other trees had very high branches. How convenient, I thought, that mine had low branches, so the leaves were easy to reach. What did he do if someone else's tree was one of the others? I didn't ask him, but I had a feeling the low-hanging tree was 'chosen' for nearly everyone.

Back at the Temple, I was seated in a small room behind the dark curtains, where I'd first seen the High Priest. A pungent smell permeated the air, seeming to come from the mats I sat on, and especially from one wall opposite me. For an instant, I thought I smelled fire burning, but then the sensation was gone. Soon a curtain parted, and a Temple Maiden came in with a steaming cup.

"The Spirit of your Tree," she whispered, "Come to lead you on your Journey of Preparation."

She sat down at the wall opposite me and watched intently as I drank. At first, the taste was bitter, but soon my tongue grew numb. Before I realized it, the brew was gone. I stared at the maiden as a strange glow appeared around her head. Her lips parted, and there was a flash like black lightning. My sight was gone—everything was black!

And then there were hands, lifting me, touching bare skin. My head whirled and visions flowed past my eyes—strange sights of stars and planets, trees, and birds flitting in and out of my sight. Physical thrills coursed through my body, and yet my mind was aching. Something felt very wrong. I tried to push clinging hands away from me, but they wouldn't leave.

Then the darkness seemed to lift, and I saw water— vast stretches such as I'd never seen before. Nothing but water, surging, rising, falling. I was tossed and tumbled helplessly. As with the blackness and the hands, there seemed to be no escape. I struggled, but there was only more water now—more and more.

At last a rock! A black piece of land loomed in the mist, and I reached out for it. But waves pushed me back, and then sent me crashing into the jagged edges. I began to fly into little pieces—bits of me everywhere, and each bit was shining like a star. Stars were beneath me in the water, and also thrown into the sky. I was scattered everywhere, and yet I existed no more.

Then, what seemed much later, I found myself on dry, hot sand. But no, I was leaning against the wall in the little room where I drank the brew. Again, my eyes tried to focus, and this time I could see that all the walls were gone except the one I leaned on. Before me yawned a great cavern, seemingly cut into the heart of the mountains. Red smudges of fire burned, and as my eyes focused more clearly, I could see there were torches hanging on the walls and little burner-lamps on a flat stone in the center of the cave. Figures in black robes were standing around this stone altar, and I saw lights dance off the headdress of the High Priest.

A sudden rustle nearby roused me further, and then I felt Feier on my shoulder.

'Are you back, Jael?' he asked.

"Yes."

'How was it?'

'Not good,' I thought to him. 'I was frightened most of the time. There were hands all over me that I couldn't stop.'

'I was afraid they might hurt you,' he said in my mind. 'Please let me stay with you for the next rituals, and I'll try to help. Remember, you do have a choice.'

I nodded, remembering the aching and longing to escape, and the nothingness of the vision when I disintegrated into stars. I hoped with all my heart Feier was right, and that I did have a choice.

Then I rose very slowly and carefully, feeling light-headed and bleary. As I did, I found a black robe around me. A great deal of swaying and chanting was going on around the altar. Next came a piercing cry, and the circle opened toward me. Almost in spite of myself, and despite Feier's claws in my shoulder, I was drawn forward into that ring of black robes.

There was a girl laid on the stone, looking much like Stephen had looked in cold death. Then my breath came in with a sharp hiss—that was my sister lying there! Only Feier's soft humming in my mind kept me from running to her. Then, as my eyes grew accustomed to the smoke, I saw her eyes were open and she was breathing very slowly. She seemed to be in some sort of trance.

"This is the Ritual of the Spirits Passed Over," the High Priest chanted ominously. "We will call the spirit Indril has sought."

He was holding a tallow lamp in one hand and in the other a small box. With a shock that moved my whole body, I recognized it as the one Martina had taken Stephen's ashes in.

Figures closed in on either side of the Priest, taking these items from his hands. The lamp then appeared somehow suspended in front of him, with the box open beside it. His hand reached into the box, as he chanted words I couldn't understand. There—right between his fingers—was all that was left of my brother. I wanted to cry out, but Feier was still humming words in my ear, telling me to keep silent. Then the Priest began to sprinkle the ashes over the flame of the lamp, and suddenly there came a blinding flash.

Directly above the table where Martina lay was a light, shimmering into the shape of a young man. But the face had no features. When it spoke, though, no one had to tell me—I knew the voice was Stephen's.

"My sister, Indril," the voice intoned, "You are called to serve The People."

As the voice continued, I could hear Feier hiss urgently in my mind, 'Be careful—don't open your mind to this.'

'But it's Stephen's voice.'

'Why would he call her Indril? That was never her name to him.'

'Well, no. But it *is* his voice.'

'Voices and sounds can be imitated.'

'But…'

'Shh. Listen, but be careful.'

"You, my sister," the voice was saying, "Are the only one left. You must carry on for all our family now. Your place and calling is here with The People."

"She's not the only one left," I whispered to Feier. "Why can't he see me?"

'Do you think Stephen would say that?'

"No!" I was talking audibly now. "He wouldn't ignore me. I'm standing right here."

Feier began to hum audibly then, a soft melody without words. Then I knew what all this meant. They had my sister in bondage to serve them, using her memory and great love for our dead brother to keep her in their grasp. 'What will they use as my great weakness?' I wondered. 'Somehow I must keep strong.'

'That's why I'm here,' Feier said, 'For strength.'

The light disappeared, and Martina was carried out by

two robed figures. The High Priest dipped his finger into a small bowl of dark liquid and began to draw a strange shape on the altar.

"And now," his voice boomed, "It is time for Stel, Child of the Sign, to be initiated into the Priesthood."

Hands guided me forward, and the Priest looked across the altar at me. His face clouded when he saw Feier, and he motioned for me to remove him from my shoulder.

"He won't leave," I said, hoping my voice didn't waver. "He's part of me."

Jah made a move to grab Feier, and suddenly the feier-cat raised his wings and let out a screech.

"He will stay." I said more confidently.

The Priest shrugged, looked down and began chanting again. One by one, the voices joined him around the circle, until I was the only one silent. Feier's humming in my ear was growing louder as the chanting increased.

"Stel!"

The High Priest's voice rang out, and total silence followed. The power of that voice pulled my eyes up to meet his. There were stars in those dark eyes, twinkling at me, as though I were looking into a piece of the night sky.

'Careful!' hissed Feier in my mind.

"You are Stel, Child of the Sign, of the Double-star. It is most sacred. And you'll be a star in the Priesthood. Your greatest desire—the very desire of your heart—is to be one with the Great Spirit."

I found myself nodding at those words as they struck a chord deep within me. It *was* my heart's desire to know God and be with him.

"But you're of a double star. You haven't released your past. You must put everything behind—forget all that you were—give up everything, even this animal you carry—you must sell your soul to the Spirit of this Place, to the Great Spirit of The People."

'Don't do it!' Feier's voice pleaded in my mind. 'Listen to how they twist the words. This Great Spirit of the People is *not* the God you seek. You must not sell your soul to them.'

Feier's words kept ringing in my mind as the Priest's voice droned on. 'You already belong to God—you and your family,' Feier said. 'The true God is love, not fear. The Spirits of these People are false and evil. They use tricks to lure people into their snares, like they used Stephen with Martina.'

Then I heard my own mind saying words back to Feier—words planted there somehow on a long-ago night, as Stephen read from the ancient book my parents kept, 'Then choose for yourselves this day whom you will serve. But as for me and my household, we will serve the Lord.'

'Yes, Jael,' Feier whispered. 'Now is the time. You must choose!'

My eyes searched the circle of robed figures. There had to be some way out. The Priests might grab me if I tried to run, but I knew Feier was right. I knew the words of The Book had held power for me before—and hoped they would help me now. If I stayed here and went along, I knew my family would end—lost in the forgetfulness of some kind of trance. If I gave up all my memory, I'd no longer know Martina, as she didn't know me. This spirit of forgetfulness couldn't be the same as the God my family talked of.

My mind became flooded with images of my two brothers, my mother, and my sister. I saw many happy moments we'd shared. Again, I saw Stephen reading from The Book, the windows tightly shuttered. 'I can't let this go!' I said to myself. 'As long as I feel a great need for this God my family believed in, it's worth trying to find him.'

Suddenly, I heard words ringing in the great cavernous room. To my surprise, they were pouring from my mouth, "I am not Stel—not a star! I am Jael, brother of Martina, Darien and Stephen. I will *not* give up myself, my identity, or my soul to anyone! There is a place, somewhere in the Universe, where I can truly be myself, and not someone else's puppet!"

As I said these words, one of the robed figures gazed at me with wondering eyes. It was so unlike the reaction of the others that I found myself speaking to him. As I paused an instant for a breath, his hood slipped slightly, and I saw a flash of blond hair. I felt sure it was Jon.

But I had to get out of there before the shock wore

off for the rest of them. I called out one last time before I turned out of the circle. "There *is* such a place, and there is a true God. I know it in my heart, and I *will* find it."

With these last words, I turned and ran for the curtains, Feier still clinging to my shoulder. We passed through a seemingly endless maze of tunnels, with no idea which one would take us out. At some of the turns, there seemed to be a bit more light or coolness in one direction or another, and we took those. Finally, we burst into open air. I expected to hear sounds of angry pursuit at any moment, but only deadly silence followed us.

CHAPTER 17

THE FIRST RAY OF LIGHT

I made my way into the mountains. There was nowhere else to go. My feet stumbled into a path that seemed vaguely familiar. Perhaps I'd seen it one day on a hunt with Daiah. I followed without really thinking, too focused on stilling my pounding heart. Feier then jumped down from my shoulder and began leading the way. He seemed to know exactly where he was going.

Soon the path climbed steeply, switching back and forth up a rock, then ending at a small cave. Crawling inside, I sat in a huddle, my head still pounding and tears beginning to blur my eyes.

'Now I've put myself in a hopeless situation. I left the City and can't go back there ever again—to them I'm nonexistent now. Even if the City is rebuilt, I don't really want to go back there. But now I've cut myself off from the Redlarks, too—even from Martina and Jon.'

Feier crawled onto my lap and licked my hand.

"Well, what now?" I asked him softly, not really expecting an answer.

'I must find Jon,' he said in my mind.

"Jon?"

'Didn't you see him—his eyes—as you spoke?'

"So that *was* Jon. But I didn't think he was a Priest."

'He was there as High Chieftain.'

"Do you think he'll help us, Feier?"

'We can only hope.'

So Feier slipped down the path, just as the sun was sinking behind the mountains above me. As the darkness settled, I felt dark and cold, inside as well as out. Pulling the thick black robe around me, I curled up in a nook at the back of the cave and tried to sleep, but my mind was too full of confusion. Between the effects of the ritual drugs and trance, and the newly-awakened burning memories of my family, I found no rest. So, I drew my knees up and sat, staring at the stone walls around me as the daylight faded. My tired mind began to wonder if I should sit in this hole in the mountains until I died. It didn't seem anyone would even miss me.

Then came the sound of footfalls and the clatter of a rock dislodged from the path. My heart jumped with fear. Had they found me so soon? Suddenly, I wanted to live again and not die. Then came a soft humming. It was Feier.

And Jon was with him. This I knew as soon as I saw the lithe form silhouetted in the cave opening. Without even stopping to think, I rushed up to him and flung my arms around him.

He stepped back, and I could see that hint of a smile, like the Jon I'd known on the ridgetop, on the journey, and not the animal I'd seen in the Duel-circle.

"So you're still fighting to live, eh Jael?" There was a low tremor in his voice.

"Just like you taught me," I nodded, trying to determine what his eyes were saying. "But now I'm also fighting to be myself—Jael—not Stel, or anyone else."

"I'm glad you are," he said, his voice going deeper. "In your courage, you've taught me a lesson."

"Me?"

"Yes. I thought you'd forget your past like everyone else does. I thought I was the only one who was strange and couldn't forget. I was ashamed and kept it a secret. But now I see you remember, too, and you've given me hope."

Suddenly Feier began batting his wings madly. 'Hurry! We must get out of the open view. I hear voices,' he hissed in my mind. And with much wing-flapping he herded us deeper into the cave.

Jon produced some food and tinder for a fire from a pouch under his cloak. But Feier warned against a fire, so we ate the cold food in darkness and silence.

The final rays of twilight faded completely as we finished eating, and I could see little of Jon's face. I was mystified. First, he'd ignored me for such a long time, making me think he'd forgotten me. Now suddenly, it was as though we were back on our journey, and none of the rest even happened. Could I trust him or not? Had he been sent by the Priests to lure me back?

Yet it was Feier who brought him, and hinted at some communications between them before this. I'd always trusted Feier, and that was all I could go on now.

Perhaps Jon was hearing some of these thoughts through Feier, for when he spoke, his voice was reassuring, "Jael, I must tell you more of my story now. I hope you'll forgive me for the times I've kept things from you. I see now that it was wrong. But I didn't know then what I know now."

"Well, I had thoughts I couldn't share with you either, but many of those were because I didn't know how to put them into words."

"Yes, I've faced that, too," he said. He lapsed into a long silence, and I wondered if he'd changed his mind. Then he took a deep breath and began to speak again, "I can tell you've learned much since our journey, and perhaps now you'll be able to understand my story better. I wish I'd known as much when I was your age."

"Right now, I feel pretty old and tired," I yawned.

"Yes, the Trance does that." He said this as though he were remembering something unpleasant. But then his voice changed, as he seemed to be pulling himself back into the present.

"Well here's some of my story," he began. "I seemed to always have trouble making up my mind. I was filled with rebellion against everyone and everything, especially after my mother died."

"What happened to her?" I asked. "They took my mother away to a place called The Institute, I think."

"Really?" he asked in surprise. "That's where my mother died. They kept trying to make her think their way, and she refused. Finally, she died from all the drugs they forced on her."

"I wonder if my mother is still alive or not," I sighed.

"They never told you?"

"Well if Stephen or Martina heard, perhaps they thought it better not to tell me."

"Now that the City has burned, we'll probably never know," he whispered. Then he continued, "Anyway, I left Terres-City for reasons you know. I was angry and wanted nothing more to do with the Council and their System. I couldn't live the way they expected—so controlled and logical. I couldn't divide myself between the day of no emotion and the dark nights of the Underground. I tried, but failed. That's why I came to the Redlarks—The People—seeking wholeness and the fulfillment of my spirit. But something is wrong here, too."

I was beginning to nod at his words now, and I moved closer to him, at last leaning against his shoulder.

"I can't put my finger on what the problem is here,

Jael. They say they've gone back to the old ways, but just because ways are old doesn't mean they're better."

"My mother once said just because ways are old doesn't necessarily mean they're bad either," I added suddenly.

"Well, perhaps that's true," Jon nodded. "The Redlarks say they live off the land and have completely left the City's technology, but when they need or want something they can't make, they steal it from the City. You saw their raiding parties on our way here."

He put his arm around my shoulders. I felt almost like I was sitting by Stephen for a moment. It had been so long.

"But those are only outward signs this place is really an outgrowth of Terres-City," he went on. "Of course, they're more receptive to the unity of body and spirit here. But they seem to be an offshoot of the Underground."

He lapsed into silence for a moment, as though he was swept along by inner thoughts. "They've released spirits here that would be better off suppressed. You've seen, I think, the fear, anger, and passion. I've been one of their worst tools. There are evil priests here, and witches."

"They deceived me, too," I said.

"I'm sorry I brought you here. I kept trying to ignore you, but you just wouldn't take no for an answer."

"It's not your fault, Jon. I needed to see this place, and find Martina. I would have come here alone if you hadn't brought me, because I'm still seeking the truth."

"To keep seeking the truth—and peace," he murmured. "Yes, I must do that, too."

His hand suddenly gripped my shoulder tightly, almost as though he was seeking support from me, rather than I from him. When he spoke again, his voice had a strange faraway tone in it, "They call you Child of the Sign, Son of the Double-Star. I called you that before I really realized it was true. Perhaps I just hoped, but no one knows what that name really means, except me. And I've known for nearly my whole life, long before the new double sun ever appeared.

"Double stars have always fascinated me, since I was much smaller than you are now. But it's more than that. It seems I've always seen everything in double—my inner self, people all around me. And it drives me crazy sometimes. Everyone seems to have two faces, one good and one evil. I keep feeling there must be some way, other than the Terres System, a way to put the two faces together in harmony. It doesn't seem right to divide the person—the mind for the day and the body for the night, always separated."

"My family said that, too," I said softly. "My brother Stephen told me there was a way for the body and mind to work together, something to do with God. But Stephen was taken from us before we learned enough from him. The Council felt we were dangerous rebels, I think. Gradually they separated us and defeated us, one by one."

I lost my voice in a sudden flood of emotion I couldn't

hold back any longer. Jon just kept his arm around me, and gently rocked a little.

"Though you wouldn't think so, it's the same here with The People," he went on. "I see the double image in myself all the more. There's part of myself that cries to do whatever the spirits will. This self wants my body's passions to rule me, to do whatever brings me pleasure, with no thought for anyone else.

But another part of me treasures what seems good and beautiful, like our friendship, Little Brother. And this part of me feels ashamed of what the spirits make me do. I see this double standard in others around me, too, though they never seem to see it. It's as though all humankind has two sides, always at war within themselves. But we all try to hide from this. I often wonder, why do I see it so clearly when no one else does?"

"I see it, Jon," I said. "I couldn't explain it, but now that you have, I see it in myself, too. Is that what it means when you say we're Children of the Double-Star?"

I felt him nod. "The Double-Star also means we can't forget our past. Oh, I tried. I'm sure you did, too. But we just don't fit here with The People. I never did, not even at the start when they first made me Chieftain. Somehow, I knew the Sign was coming, long before it came. It gave a good excuse to return to the City, too. But that didn't help me, either. I was torn between two selves, and two places—wanting each one whenever I was in the other, and if truth be told, not really wanting either one. But I could see no other choice."

"I know, Jon." My voice trailed off, failing me, but I knew now he understood.

"But you and Feier have opened my eyes and my mind," he said suddenly. "He tells me to follow my heart and choose for myself. And you've shown me that maybe—somewhere out there in the Universe—there's another choice for us."

"A place where we can truly be ourselves," I said wistfully. "A place where love is real, and the mind and body are not divided."

"Jael, you've shown me love is the key. You stood firm because of your love for your family. No one I've seen in the City or the Redlarks has this kind of love."

Suddenly it was as though a light flashed in my mind. "Yes!" I heard my voice cry. "I remember words my mother read to me. I was so small, but they're here in my mind, still clear. 'God is love. Let us love one another. He who loves is born of God and knows God.' Why didn't I remember sooner? Why doesn't anyone else on Terres understand this? Jon, we must find somewhere where they do understand this idea, that God is love. We need to learn more about this, so we can find the true God."

Jon grabbed my hand. "I knew we were thinking the same way. We must go together, and search."

"But where do we go?"

"Well, we know there's no hope on this side of the Peaks," he said, looking toward the cave's entrance. "I think we must go to whatever lies on the other side."

"That's like going over the edge of the world." My heart was racing now, in mingled fear and excitement. "But what's over there?"

"I've only seen it once, from the top of the highest peak. They call it the Far Wilds, where no man lives. It seemed just a great empty plain as far as I could see. But what other choice do we have?"

I reached for his hand and squeezed it tightly as the next question came to my mind, "What about Martina?"

"We must leave her, I think," he sighed. "She's already forgotten everything, even her name. It's too late for her."

"No!" I cried suddenly, not caring how loud I was. "I won't leave my sister in such bondage. She's my family, and I won't give up hope."

I jumped up, turned, and glared into his eyes. "You're the High Chieftain! She's your Consort, you say. Surely there's something you can do?"

Abruptly my voice left me, and I crumpled to the hard stone floor. Jon pulled me to him gently, rubbing my back. For an instant, I was taken back in long-lost time, back to when my father used to sing me to sleep. I could almost hear the song he used – *"Oh Danny Boy…"* But there was silence except for our breathing.

"I tried to warn you from the start, Jael."

"I know, but love keeps on fighting to live, too."

"You know, I never realized that before."

"Perhaps there's some way to bring her back with love," I added.

"You've taught me a lot about love, Jael. If anything can save her—though I'm not sure it can—the only chance is your great love for her."

After this his voice trailed off, and he seemed to be deep in thought.

I sat up again, watching as light from one of the rising moons touched his form. Finally, he looked up, and I asked, "Do you have a plan?"

"Yes. In two days, the camps will gather for the Ritual of the Goddess."

"Isn't that one of their fertility rites?" I interrupted. "I read about them. They're full of passion and all kinds of—well, orgies. How can you do such things?"

"I don't want to, Jael. But at the moment, we have no other choice. Please let me finish."

"I'm sorry," I muttered. "I just hope this idea works."

"Well, it's the only one I have right now. As High Chieftain, my Consort and I must initiate the Ritual-"

Again, I found myself interrupting, "You and my sister?" My mind filled with memories of the way she and Jon had looked at each other after the Duel, and I felt a little sick.

"Jael," he began again, softly. "Please try to understand.

I must do this if we're to get her to come with us. To her I'm just another man now. But I find I *am* beginning to care for her in a different way. I'll try to communicate your love for her through myself."

The tone in his voice soothed my nerves. I realized now there was no hint of the animal I'd seen in the Duel. "Okay," I said.

"All right. Here's the plan. I'll fake the Trance, so I can somehow sneak her away. You'll wait above us on the trail up the mountains where they're not so high. Our camp will move tomorrow, so you must follow at a safe distance."

It all sounded unreal to me, but I could see no other choice. After that night, and all our talking, I was beginning to regain my trust in Jon. But perhaps that was because I just needed someone, and he was all I had. Soon he returned to the camp, and I tried to sleep.

***

For the next few days, I hardly ate or slept. I was on the move, but even if this hadn't been the case, I was too full of fear and anticipation. As the camp took portable shelters and moved south, Feier scented their trail and followed at a safe distance, with me close behind him.

I had no trouble finding Jon's trail to the mountain pass. Then after spending a day of searching, I found what seemed to be the best spot from which to observe the new camp unseen, in a saddle directly above the sweeping valley at the base of the mountains. There was great activity below for the next full day, as more camps arrived—the setting up of bark-shelters, building of fires, and much shouting, chanting, and dancing. In the center of the camp, a brightly colored fabric tent was put up with wood supports on a large wooden platform.

Just after sunrise the next morning, the Ritual of the Goddess began. Martina was led from her shelter by two maidens, already in the Trance. Then two men brought Jon to join her at the steps to the platform. My heart sank when I saw him. He looked like he was deep in the Trance, too. What if his plan failed? Or had he forgotten about me?

I felt very cold and alone up on that mountain as they stood there, The People throwing flowers over their heads and sprinkling some kind of liquid on them. Then the chanting swelled, and I could see them starting up the steps. I strained my eyes with the distance, and colors began to run together. The curtain of the pavilion parted, and then dropped behind them.

Now my heart failed. It suddenly occurred to me there was no other exit to that wall tent. If they came out now, they'd be seen. I was sure Jon had betrayed me.

But then something began to happen which I hadn't expected. As soon as Jon and Martina disappeared, a great cheering arose and all The People began rushing about, grabbing each other and dashing off, laughing and screaming, into shelters and out among the trees. Soon there wasn't one soul left in the clearing.

Jon didn't fail me, after all. Soon I could see him creeping slowly up the path towards me. I raced Feier out to greet them. Martina, still in the Trance, had no idea where she was, and didn't seem to care. But she kept pace as we climbed steadily upward.

My mind was too full of wondering what lay ahead to look much at the scene around me. Great walls of rock rose above us for most of the day, changing colors as the sun rose and crossed the sky. Our path was quite steep, but it was really a mild slope compared to many of the surrounding rock faces.

So we toiled throughout that day, pausing often to rest. The sun dipped behind the Peaks just as we reached the top of the pass. But when we crossed the divide, I was amazed to find the sun ahead of us, still well above the horizon. I hadn't realized before that the sun didn't really set when it went behind the mountains. Now it lighted a great flat plain below us which seemed to stretch forever. We had enough daylight left to start down and find shelter in a grove of trees for the night.

We even built a fire, for Jon felt sure no one would pursue us. "They won't even miss us until it's time to return to the main camp in two days."

That night I settled down to sleep feeling hopeful for the first time in a long time. But sometime in the night, a terrible howling sound woke me. I sat bolt upright, thinking some fearsome animal was near us. Then I saw, by the fading embers of the fire, Martina grabbing and clawing at Jon.

"Where am I?" she screamed. Then she let out that howl again. "What have you done to me? I should be with The People!"

The sound of her cry made me shudder through my whole body. Somehow Jon managed to quiet her, but I could still see fires burning in her eyes. She looked like a frightened animal.

I lay back down, feeling very depressed. Would I ever get my sister back from her bondage?

It was late when the sun finally came over the shadow of the mountains and shone on our camp. I felt very weary, and my limbs didn't seem to want to move. At last, I raised my head and saw Jon standing nearby, over what looked like a pile of blankets. As I rose, I saw it was Martina, huddled into a ball and rocking herself slowly like a child. She was moaning softly and occasionally cried out in words I couldn't understand.

When Jon saw me, he came and put his arm over my shoulder. "She's been like this most of the night," he said. "Now is the time for your love's greatest battle."

I really don't remember all that went on through the day. We stayed in our camp and tried to talk to her, as the sun crossed the sky. Sometimes tears would overcome me, and I'd walk to the edge of the trees, looking up to see Regelian and its twin, two bright eyes trying to blind me. 'Why do I have to be a Child of the Sign?' I wondered. 'How much easier if I could've just forgotten like everyone else. Well, Jon didn't forget either. At least I have his friendship. But will my sister ever remember me?' My heart was filling with despair.

It was almost evening as I stood watching the light fade. Jon brought some coarse bread and berry-leather to me. "You should eat something," he said softly.

"Oh yeah, my favorite food!" I tried to laugh. It tasted like dust in my mouth.

When I came back into our camp, I was surprised to see Martina sitting up and looking at Jon. Her eyes seemed to be focusing on him now, instead of just staring blankly.

"Why do you deprive me of my life?" she asked in a low angry voice.

'At least I can understand her words now,' I thought.

"And why do you call me that name, Martina? I am Indril! I've never been another. And my brother Stephen— my only brother—you took me from him, too!" Suddenly she lunged at Jon, trying to claw his face.

Jon grabbed her arms and pinned her to the ground. Not since the Duel had I seen him react so quickly.

"You've spoken," he said between clenched teeth. "Now you'll listen to truth. I'm still your Chieftain, you're still my Consort, and you *will* obey me."

"I reject you!" she screamed, spitting in his face.

Then Feier jumped on my shoulder suddenly and hissed in my ear, 'You must use love, not force. Use your love, Jael.'

I moved closer to them and cried, "You *are* Martina! You're my sister, and I love you."

A puzzled look came over her face as she turned to stare at me.

"You're Stel, Child of the Sign."

"Child of the Sign, yes—because I can't forget my past. But my name is Jael."

Jon let go of her, and now she reached her hand toward me. I could see it shaking. "Jael?" she asked in a whisper.

"Yes, your little brother." My voice began to quiver. "Once you said I looked like Stephen."

Her hand was touching my hair now.

Then Jon's voice came quietly. "They kept you in bondage, Martina. They used your weakness and gave you a voice that sounded like Stephen, but it was only an illusion. Here you can return to reality. You can look into your true brother's eyes. Which is worth more to you?"

"Jael?" she repeated. Then she shook her head. "Somewhere in a dream, you were there. And Darien."

"Yes, we have another brother named Darien. He went with the Inland Raiders. We could try to find him and be a family again."

I moved closer to her now, holding her hand. Her

other hand was in my hair, moving down my face, touching my eyes, and then my lips. Suddenly it was as if a wave broke, like the one crashing against the rock in my vision. But this time the result was not scattering stars, but a smile on her face, along with tears in her eyes.

"Jael!" There was a new tone in her voice now. "Yes, I remember. Stephen *is* in your eyes. How could I have left you? Please forgive me, Jael. I love you."

We fell into each other's arms, sobbing with joy.

That night I slept better than I had for a very long time. All of us did.

With the first light, Jon woke us and we prepared to journey into the Far Wilds. We had no idea what lay ahead for us, but to me it didn't matter now. I had Martina back, and this was like that first ray of light flooding my black bedroom so long ago, when I was a frightened child.

CHAPTER 18

THE STARS ALWAYS SHINE

The lamp's light was slowly fading, its shapes and figures disappearing. Soon the only light in the room was from the single candle on the coffee table.

"I feel like we've been gone a long time, on a great journey," Ginna sighed.

"In a sense, we have," came Jon's quiet voice.

"Well, what do you think now?" Jael asked. "Have we offered any help?"

There was a long silence, filled with thoughts of how to explain feelings that were without expression.

It was Danny who finally spoke, "I'm not sure really," he began. "But I do feel something has happened inside me. I feel different."

"I feel stronger," Ginna added, "And not as afraid."

"But what do we do now?" asked Danny. "There's still the problems at school."

"Just use the new strength you spoke of," Jael replied.

"God doesn't give us the answers all at once. But as you walk with him one step at a time, each next step will become clearer."

"I sure hope so," sighed Ginna.

"Perhaps it's the way your troubles, Jael and Jon, make ours seem small by comparison," Danny continued.

"And you've helped me see there's always hope, no matter how terrible things seem," added Ginna.

"Yes," Danny cut in. "Like the saying that there's always light at the end of the tunnel."

Jon nodded at this. "In our time people say, 'On the darkest night, the stars still shine'."

"Just like Jael's light in his room when he was lost. It filled his heart with hope when he needed it most."

"That's right," Ginna cried. "And this was the same light he felt in his heart when Martina came back to him."

"I hope you've felt it, too," Jael said, "That love is real and it brings hope."

"Is this where the story says, 'And they all lived happily ever after'?" Danny asked.

Jael laughed softly, "Hardly! Not in the Far Wilds."

"There were continued trials we all had to face. We still had much to learn, and the same will be true for you," Jon said. "But we'd reached a turning point. I hope you'll find the same. True stories never really end with 'happily ever after' you know."

"Except when we get to Heaven," said Ginna.

"But those are other tales for other times," Jael said. "This is the story for you now—the story of light, love and hope. As I said, the real light of hope for us was when we both discovered the great power of love."

"And that God is Love, right?"

"Exactly, Ginna," Jon nodded. "God is always there to help and give hope, if we just call on him."

"That's what we should remember then," Danny said, after a moment's silence.

Jon and Jael nodded silently. Then there was a rustling sound, and the candle flame rose. Looking up, Danny and Ginna could see their visitors standing and smiling at them.

"Do you have to leave?" Danny pleaded.

"It's time," came Jon's voice. "But we may meet again, when there's need—when you call."

"Can we call you anytime we want to?" Danny asked.

"Your call isn't something you're aware of, just like this time," Jon answered. "If you try consciously to call, it won't happen. Only when the call comes from your heart, beyond your mind, will we be able to come. It will happen when it's *meant* to, not necessarily when you *want* it to."

"Oh," sighed Danny.

"No, don't be discouraged," said Jael. "This just means when you need us most, we *will* come. But not until then."

"And remember, the Lord-God is always with you," Jon added. "That's the most precious thing you can ever ask for—and you have it, I know."

By this time, the four of them were moving slowly toward the back door. As they stepped through, Ginna and Danny weren't surprised to see it was dark. It seemed very late, perhaps almost midnight, and stars were shining brilliantly overhead in their familiar constellation patterns.

"Is this the same night you came?" Ginna asked softly. "It seems like years have passed."

"Within you, perhaps they have," Jon whispered. "But in your world's time, it's been only a matter of hours. You see, we've all been in the GAP."

For a moment, all four of them gazed in silence at the blazing lights of the stars.

"They seem so far away," Jael said at last.

"They are," said Jon. "We're far from the center of the Galaxy here." He looked at Ginna and Danny intently for a moment, then went on, "Here's another way to remember the Lord-God is always with you. The stars are always there—always shining—whether it's the light of day or the darkest night. A stronger light, like the sun, may hide them for a time, or clouds can block them from your view. But they're *always* there. Remember that."

Then he turned, looked up at the sky again, and didn't speak anymore.

"Farewell, Ginna and Daniel." Jael grasped each of their hands briefly.

They looked into his shining eyes, but could find no words to speak.

Jael handed the candle to Danny, blowing it out as he did so. Then he turned away, and with Jon, began walking down the porch steps, across the backyard, and toward the west.

Gradually the two dark silhouettes rose against the sky. Then in the blink of an eye, they were gone. And in their place, were only the stars—always shining.

Ginna couldn't say how long they stood in silence there, just gazing at the empty horizon and the sky full of stars. Time seemed to have lost all meaning.

The sound of a car and the crunch of gravel came, and they recognized the hum of that engine immediately.

"Mom's home," she whispered.

"Yeah."

Danny reached over and took her hand. At his touch, she turned and their eyes met. For a moment, she could have sworn she saw that sky full of stars right there in her brother's eyes.

"Do you think we dreamed it all?" she asked, barely audible.

"Whether we did or not, it's part of us now. Even dreams have something important to teach us," he replied.

For an instant, he sounded more like Jael than her little brother. Then his voice changed, and he was just Danny again. "Besides, Ginna, how could we both have the same dream?"

She found no words to reply.

"Come on," he added, "We'd better go in now."

She nodded, "And tell Mom we've been looking at the stars."

PREVIEW OF
THE PEAKS SAGA, BOOK 2

"SEARCHING FOR MAIA"

CHAPTER 1

DUST IN THE WIND

Danny Parker stood at the window listening to the mournful howl of the wind. When was it ever going to stop? He felt their old house shudder with the strongest gusts. Looking down at the windowsill, he saw the layer of fine, black dust getting thicker. These old windows just couldn't keep it out.

'I'll have to clean this place again,' he sighed to himself. 'No one else will.'

His mother was still working long hours in her public relations job at the big nuclear power plant outside of town. 'You'd think with all the hours she puts in, we'd be able to afford a better house by now,' he mused. 'But Mom says it's still too hard to make ends meet, since Dad isn't sending the child support he was supposed to.' This made him angry, though he didn't want to feel this way about his father.

So, five years after they'd come to this small town in eastern Colorado, they were still living in the little, rickety house that had been "only temporary."

The reverberations of a deep bass rhythm were rising from his sister Ginna's room. Every day after school, all she did was retreat into her room and play loud music. Now that she was almost out of high school, so many things had changed between them. They just didn't communicate like they used to. They'd been very close in grade school, but now they seemed to be drawing farther apart with each passing day.

Danny sighed and began tracing patterns in the dust on the windowsill. He felt a lump rising in his throat and tried desperately to swallow it. 'I'm too old to cry!' he told himself. 'I'm almost fourteen years old. I have to be the man of this house now that Dad is gone for good.'

Despite his efforts, tears were already trickling down his cheeks. Two of them dropped into the dust on the sill and spread into strange patterns. Looking down through tear-blurred eyes, he blinked at the picture he saw. His finger had drawn a jagged line like a range of mountains. The tear shapes looked like two figures walking toward him out of a haze.

Yes, that really happened once, though it was over four years ago now, and seemed like forever. Jon and Jael came to them out of time—what they called the GAP. Jael shared the story of his life with them, and they found hope and strength to face their trials in this new home. But now that seemed so long ago. The hope he and Ginna once felt seemed to have dried up and blown away, with the dust in the wind out here on the barren plains.

Suddenly a terribly strong gust shook the house. Afraid the window might blow in, Danny stepped back, covering his face with his arm. When he looked at the window again, two blond figures were standing there, gazing into his eyes.

"Ginna!" he cried. "They're back!"

His sister poked her head out her bedroom door. "Who's back?" she demanded. "What are you bugging me for?"

"Jon and Jael are here," he said, trying to keep his voice from wavering.

The two figures smiled at him and stepped aside to reveal a third figure standing just behind them. This one was a girl only slightly taller than Jael. Her dark brown hair hung long and straight to her shoulders, and her deep green eyes seemed to flash as she glanced over at Ginna, who'd just stepped out of her door.

"I'm Martina Sullien, Jael's sister," she said. "We came at your call, Daniel and Virginia."

"Don't call me that! My name is Ginna! And what did you have to call them for, anyway? Do we need another lecture on hope and faith?"

Danny flinched noticeably at her words. "I'm sorry," he said to the three standing before him. "She's just not herself lately."

"Maybe I'm finally learning to be myself for a change," said Ginna, stepping closer to them now.

"Perhaps you are, Ginna," came Martina's voice, very calm and even. "I know how difficult that can be, believe me."

Something in her manner seemed to calm Ginna. "I'm sorry," she murmured. "It's so strange to see Jon and Jael here. I'd almost decided it was all just a dream. It seems so long ago now." Her voice tapered into a wistful tone.

"Time is a very relative thing," said Jon. "Who can say what time has done in its many flowing directions since last we talked?"

"I can see that Daniel is taller," Jael said. "He's almost as tall as I am."

"So he is," Jon agreed. "Now, why have you both called us this time?"

"You mean I called, too?" Ginna asked incredulously.

"It appears so, since Martina is here," said Jon.

"Well, I think you can guess why I called," said Danny, glancing at Ginna out of the corner of his eye. "We just don't seem to be communicating the way we used to. Something has come between us."

"Or perhaps something is missing between you," said Martina softly.

"Well, I guess it could be that," Ginna whispered. She was standing next to Danny now, her eyes still fixed on Martina. "Why do I feel I know you already?" she asked at last.

"Our lives may have touched before without our knowing it," Martina replied.

"But how?"

"Is she a forerunner, too?" Danny asked.

"Not exactly," Jon replied. "It's more complicated than that. When we were here before, we told you we were from the future because it was the simplest explanation. But that isn't completely accurate. Let me try another way. Have you heard of parallel universes?"

"No," said Danny.

"I have," Ginna said. "In physics class. Worlds that are sort of next to ours, but we can't see them. One is positive, and the other negative."

"Some are opposites like that, but not all," Jon smiled. He turned to the blinds on the window beside them. "Here's a simple way to explain it. These blinds are colored on one side, white on the other, right? He closed the blinds.

They both nodded.

"This blue side represents your world," he said. "You see only this side. If we were on the other side, we'd see only our world, just the white side."

"I get it!" cried Danny. "When they're opened just the right amount, we can see both sides at once—both worlds."

"That's right, Daniel."

"So when we see you, our worlds are touching," mused Ginna, "The blinds are open."

"Not only when you see us," said Martina. "Sometimes you sense us with other senses than sight."

"And sometimes you can just feel our presence subconsciously without realizing it," Jael added.

"But I sure haven't felt you lately," said Danny. "It's been really lonely around here."

Ginna glared at him. "Well, it's not all my fault."

"Wait," said Jon quietly. "We've come to help as much as we can."

"Are you going to tell us more of your story, Jael?" asked Danny.

"Jon is the story-teller this time," said Jael.

"Yes, now you'll get to see my point of view," Jon nodded. "But I'm not going to just tell you this time. I'm going to take you with me through the blinds to my world. That is, if you're willing to come."

"But how?" Ginna demanded.

"As Jael and Martina," he said softly.

"You mean in their bodies? That's impossible!" she cried.

"I love that word impossible," Jon smiled. "Haven't you read, 'With God, all things are possible'?"

"But I don't want to be lost in someone else's body," she said. "What if we can't come back?"

"It's all right, Ginna," said Danny suddenly, looking into Jael's eyes. "Jael and I have touched many times before, I think. At times, we're almost the same person."

"Remember, we live in parallel worlds," Jon added. "This wouldn't work, otherwise."

"You mean in this world I'm Ginna, but in yours I'm Martina?"

"That's one way to explain it," the tall blond nodded.

"Then right now, am I talking to myself? Looking at myself?"

"Is this any different from looking at yourself in a mirror or talking to yourself when you're alone?"

"Well, I guess it's not. But I'm still afraid," Ginna finally admitted.

Martina stepped forward, taking her hand. "We're all a little afraid of ourselves sometimes, afraid of what we'll find hidden in the deepest recesses of our minds. But it's much better to face those fears and let them flow past us. Then we can learn and move on."

Now Jael stepped forward and took Danny's hand. "Will you do it?" he asked.

"Yes," Danny nodded.

Ginna gave a wordless nod, too.

"Everyone join hands in a circle," Jon said. "And close your eyes."

Even with their eyes closed, they saw a honey-colored light begin to glow in the center of the circle, its warmth radiating toward them, then flowing through them. One moment, Danny was standing between Jael and Martina, with Ginna between Martina and Jon. Then Jael seemed to be gone. Danny found himself holding a larger, stronger hand. It could only be Jon's.

The honey-colored light filled the room now. Someone looking in through the open blinds would have seen three figures standing in a circle, bathed in the rich light. Then the light seemed to flow out of the window, through the blinds, and the figures were gone.

Thank you!

Thank you for joining me. If you liked the story and have a minute to spare, I would appreciate a short comment on the page or site where you bought the book.

Reviews from readers like you make a huge difference to helping new readers find stories similar to *Peaks at the Edge of the World*.

- Amazon
- Barnes & Noble
- Goodreads
- iBooks

Thank you!

M. F. Erler

ABOUT THE AUTHOR

M.F. Erler has been writing since she was about 14 years old. In fact, some of the initial ideas and characters for "The Peaks at the Edge of the World" were conceived when she was in high school, while writing assignments for freshman English class. Her lifelong goal has been to get the Peaks Trilogy out to readers, and thanks to new developments in electronic publishing, her dream has been fulfilled.

Fantasy and Science Fiction have long been among her favorite reading materials, and her favorite authors are C.S. Lewis and J.R.R. Tolkien. She is also interested in history, comparative religion, ecology, and music. Her previous publications include non-fiction articles in "Today's Christian Parent" and "Social Studies and the Young Learner." She has worked as an Environmental

Education teacher and facilitator, and also as a music teacher. Hobbies include reading, playing several musical instruments, and needlework.

She and her husband, Paul, have two adult children. All make their home in the Pacific Northwest.

Contact Frances at mferler@peaksandbeyond.com
Or follow her blog at PeaksAndBeyond.com

CPSIA information can be obtained
at www.ICGtesting.com
Printed in the USA
FFHW01n1930230818
48007152-51707FF

9 781937 333614